A marriage on paper only...

All of Joe's doubts about the wedding hit him with stunning force when he turned and saw Sable walking toward him and the minister.

She was beautiful. And she was his. Not to touch. Just to give her his name. He had even signed a contract to that effect.

This is a business marriage, he tried to convince himself....

Joe didn't hear a word of the ceremony until the minister reached the part he'd been waiting for—the kiss.

He lifted Sable's veil and stared into eyes that were as uncertain as his. *Just a short kiss*, he promised himself.

But when his lips touched hers, every muscle in his body tightened to the breaking point. Joe forgot everything except the pleasure of kissing his wife, pulling her closer, fitting her slender frame to his own hard body.

Only a kiss to seal the bargain? the voice inside him mocked. Joe raised his head and stared at his bride—a woman he barely knew.

He was trapped. And right now he didn't give a damn.

Rita Clay Estrada, cofounder and first president of the Romance Writers of America, didn't start out to be a writer. She studied art and psychology, worked as a model, a secretary, a salesperson and a bookstore manager. But when Rita began to write, the results were explosive—*To Buy a Groom* is her ninth Temptation. A true romantic, Rita has taken a beloved story line—the marriage of convenience—and written a dramatic, emotion-filled love story that begins after the hero and heroine say "I do." This talented author makes her home in Texas.

Books by Rita Clay Estrada

HARLEQUIN TEMPTATION
48–THE WILL AND THE WAY
72–A WOMAN'S CHOICE
100–SOMETHING TO TREASURE
136–THE BEST THINGS IN LIFE
166–THE IVORY KEY
188–A LITTLE MAGIC
220–TRUST
265–SECOND TO NONE

Don't miss any of our special offers. Write to us at the following address for information on our newest releases.

Harlequin Reader Service
901 Fuhrmann Blvd., P.O. Box 1397, Buffalo, NY 14240
Canadian address: P.O. Box 603,
Fort Erie, Ont. L2A 5X3

To Buy
a Groom
RITA CLAY ESTRADA

Harlequin Books

TORONTO • NEW YORK • LONDON
AMSTERDAM • PARIS • SYDNEY • HAMBURG
STOCKHOLM • ATHENS • TOKYO • MILAN

For F.P.S., who showed me the way,
and for good friends Diane Levitt, Faye Ashley,
Pat Leonard and Mom.

Published September 1990

ISBN 0-373-25413-X

1

JOSEPH LOMBARDI hated horses. No, he amended, he hated taking care of horses. He loved horse racing. He was trying to decide which emotion was stronger, when a soft voice interrupted.

"Mr. Lombardi? Mr. Joseph Lombardi?"

"Yes," he answered, annoyed. He continued to examine his prize thoroughbred's hoof.

"I'm Sable LaCroix. I have an appointment with you." Her voice was low and slightly hesitant, but the words were a reminder, just the same. "One of your men said you were out here in the stables."

Joe sighed heavily, dropped Ahab's hoof and patted the horse's neck before turning around. Mrs. LaCroix was another problem in a day filled with them. He'd deliberately avoided the appointment. He didn't have time for wealthy socialites with strange requests for meetings without a stated purpose.

The barn filtered sunlight and shadows, and the woman standing inside the entrance seemed to gather both around her like a silver cloak. She was tall, probably about five foot seven or eight without her heels. Her figure was breathtaking. Full breasts, softly rounded hips and long, slender legs. Beautiful. Very beautiful.

And from what he could see, she was dark-headed—his weakness.

"I remember now, Mrs. LaCroix. My attorney said you're looking for an investment for your dead husband's money. Right?"

He saw her wince at his crass words. "Right."

"And you thought horse racing in Texas was right up your alley, since racetracks and betting will be here in a matter of months."

"Right."

He took off his hat and wiped his face on his sleeve. "Fine. Then do some more talking to my attorney. Mike can handle everything."

She shifted her weight onto one hip; the movement made her legs look longer than ever. "This can't be handled by attorneys. There are some strings attached that *you* have to deal with," she said, her voice melodic, like a gentle waterfall.

Her white suit was crisp and cool. Just looking at her made him feel as if a soft, Southern breeze had touched his skin. A wide-brimmed, black hat shaded her eyes, so he couldn't see their color. His eyes dropped again to her long legs, legs that were designed to be kissed all the way up to . . . Damn! Not liking his reaction to her, Joe made his voice hard. "What strings? And what makes you think I might be interested? I have a lot of work to do. Make it quick."

She hesitated for only a moment. "I need a husband with a good background and a stable career. You need money. I'm willing to offer you a million dollars on the day of the wedding."

Joe stared at her blankly, then shook his head. Obviously the heat was affecting his hearing.

He saw her nod. She must have read his expression. "You heard correctly, Mr. Lombardi." Her voice held a hint of amusement. "I'm asking for your hand in marriage."

That was it. He threw his head back and laughed, slapping the hat against his leg. Her proposal was the stupidest thing he'd ever heard, but at least it was funny.

He became aware that his visitor was patiently waiting for his laughter to stop. Her stance relaxed, a smile played at the corners of her beautiful lips.

His laughter slowly died. He narrowed his eyes. His lips tightened. "Lady, you aren't kidding, are you?"

"No. I'm not kidding."

"Why?"

"I need a husband. You need an investor for the new track you want to build."

Gripping Ahab's lead, he walked the horse out of the barn toward the nearest paddock. It was always best to ignore drunks and crazies, no matter how beautiful they might be. He wasn't sure which category she fitted into and he wasn't about to find out.

Joe opened the paddock gate and led the thoroughbred inside before unsnapping the lead. After a swat on the hindquarter the horse trotted away as Joe exited.

Aware that the beautiful stranger had followed him, Joe turned toward her. Her businesslike demeanor was betrayed by her tight grip on the black-and-white clutch purse, he noted. Did it hold the million she was trying to bribe him with? After hearing her offer, he thought she might be stupid enough to carry it with her.

"I repeat, Mrs. LaCroix. Why?"

"Because I need a respectable husband and the semblance of a family life. You can give me that."

Her claim intrigued him. Silently he led her to his rambling ranch home. He'd listen to her—very politely, just like his daddy had taught him—and then he'd kick her out on her little butt. Her very enticing little butt.

Allowing her to enter the kitchen before him, his eyes lingered on that very appealing part of her anatomy. She turned to face him. "Mr. Lombardi?"

His eyes darted to her face. One brow was raised as if in demand. He might as well get this interview over with. "Who sent you here?"

"Would you believe my husband?"

"No."

"He did. You remember John LaCroix in Vietnam? You two were buddies, trapped in the same section of the jungle. Then after you were wounded, you were roommates in the hospital. He mentioned you often. I've even read the letters you two exchanged for a while, after you both returned home. John said you were the most dependable man he'd ever known—always willing to help."

His eyes widened at the flash of memory. He and John LaCroix had been two disillusioned, eighteen-year-old kids, wondering what had happened to the glory of war and pride in defending one's country. They had been the best of friends, until the normalcy of life returned once more and soothed their nightmares. "You're that LaCroix's wife?"

She nodded. In the sunlight he saw her eyes were brown. Big and round and brown. As soft as a doe's hide.

"For three years," she answered.

"Then what happened?"

"He died."

John was gone. Joe could hardly believe it.

She pulled out a kitchen chair and slid gratefully into it, almost as if she'd been carrying a heavy weight. Lifting the wide-brimmed hat off her head, she tossed it onto the table.

He wanted to moan—both in delight and frustration. Her hair was the exact color of her name—Sable.

"It's funny, isn't it?" she said bitterly. "He lived through everything war could throw at him. Then he died in an airplane crash, trying to make it home in time for our son's first birthday party."

Hands stuffed in his back pockets, Joe stared at her. Somehow none of this seemed real. She was mourning for a lost husband; he was sorry about the boy he had known so long ago. "I'm sorry," he finally said, awkwardly. "I didn't know. He was an all right guy."

Anger flashed in her eyes and her back stiffened. The reaction was short-lived, and she slumped back into her chair. "Yes. But he was more than that. He was a wonderful, compassionate man."

"When did it happen?"

"A little over two years ago."

Memories he thought he'd buried, surfaced, quick and sure, cutting to his heart. So many friends had been lost. And the worst of it was that afterward it was hard to remember what had been real and what had been just a nightmare. He'd forgotten those feelings, but he hadn't forgotten John.

Now John's widow was sitting with him, trying to talk him into taking John's place. It left a bad taste in his mouth. People didn't replace other people.

"So you're looking for a replacement for this wonderful, compassionate man," he jeered, trying to quell his conflicting emotions. "Well, sorry, lady, but I'm not either one of those things. I don't like wives and I'm not partial to kids. Now if you'd given birth to a thoroughbred—"

"I did."

"What?"

"The LaCroix name and wealth are very well-known. They're fourth-generation Louisianans, with enough money to buy the state." She leaned back, closing her eyes for a moment, letting her guard down enough for him to see how tired she was. When she opened her eyes he almost fell into their soft, brown depths. "And I own thoroughbreds, Mr. Lombardi. Three, compliments of my husband's estate."

He leaned against the chair in front of him, baring his teeth as he smiled. "Your in-laws are very generous to want to help John's old buddy by setting him up with their son's widow." He couldn't help the sarcastic tone. This whole conversation was ridiculous, yet here he was, when he had a hundred other things to do!

"No," she said, so quietly he had to strain himself to hear her. "They want my son."

He felt the sadness, the loneliness in her voice, but it was no concern of his. "Why would two old people want a youngster? They certainly couldn't take care of him properly."

"They want him as another LaCroix possession, but they'll only make him weak and worthless. John fought against them, and so will I. They wrapped John in cotton batting until he almost suffocated from their love. I don't want that to happen to my child."

This deserved a drink. He reached into the refrigerator and pulled out a beer, popped the top and guzzled, then wiped his mouth on his sleeve. "What do you want me to do, lady? Fight them off with my bare hands?"

"I want you to be a respectable husband, so my child can have a complete family—a mother and a father. Then the LaCroix can't take me to court and sue for custody of my son."

"You're kidding!"

"Mr. Lombardi," she said slowly, patiently. "My attorney contacted your attorney last week. Didn't he even mention why I wanted to see you?"

"Not a word, lady. Not one damn word." Why hadn't Mike said something? He'd been out at the ranch only yesterday, hemming and hawing about money and how much it was going to take for Joe to get the track and stables ready for the racing season. But he hadn't actually *said* anything—just mentioned in passing to come by the office next time Joe was in town, because he might have a solution....

"You're the solution," Joe muttered, tightening his grip around the beer can until the sound of popping aluminum filled the air. Beer spilled over his hand and dripped to the floor, but he ignored it. He was staring at the woman seated at his table, the woman who looked as if she nibbled on exotic flowers for breakfast.

Sable looked startled. "The solution to your money problems? Yes, I suppose I am. Just as you're the answer to mine. If you want my horses as well, you can have them. I need a husband."

Joe tossed the can into the sink on top of the breakfast dishes, which were on top of the dinner dishes that hadn't been done the night before. The place was a mess. Every square inch of counter was covered with dirty dishes, pots and pans. But the table was clean. He was particular about where he ate his thrown-together meals.

"Look," he began, hoping he sounded reasonable. "I'm sorry you're having problems with your in-laws, but I'm sure if you talk to them, explain to them, they'll see things your way. A child needs his mama. Grandparents aren't always young or energetic enough to raise a little guy. They'd be worn out in a month."

"Wrong. They'll do anything to gain custody. I heard them." She stood, bracing both exquisitely manicured hands on the table and leaned toward him to make her point. "They want him because he's a LaCroix. They won't raise him, just indoctrinate him with cute little phrases like, 'A LaCroix would never work for charity, just donate to it.' Then they'll give him to someone else to raise and bring him downstairs from the nursery to show off to their friends. The same way my husband was raised. He hated it. I hate it, too." She straightened and stared him straight into his baby blues. "I want him because he's *my* son. *My* child. I want to be there when he goes to school, falls down playing ball, swims his first lap across a pool."

She reached for her purse and hat. "But if you don't want to get involved in this, then fine. Not everyone is afraid of money. I'll find someone else to help me."

He watched her walk out of the kitchen and down the hallway toward the front door. That tight butt swayed from side to side.

"Who?" The word was out before he even realized he'd thought it.

She turned, her hand on the doorknob. Her eyes had to be the saddest, brownest eyes he'd ever made the mistake of losing himself in. "I don't know yet, Mr. Lombardi. But I'll find someone who needs my money as much as I need his help. I guess John was wrong about you."

Then she opened the front door and walked out, closing it quietly behind her.

Joe stood rooted to the foot of the stairs, his eyes still trained on the spot she had occupied. A powerful engine revved in the driveway, then the sound diminished as she drove away.

Had he dreamed her? He wasn't sure. But if he was dreaming, at least he'd fantasized about someone beautiful. She was drop-dead gorgeous. And she was trouble.

Shaking his head at her outrageous request, he walked out to the barn. He had too much work to do and not enough time to get it done.

SABLE PULLED OVER to the side of the dirt road and leaned her head on the steering wheel. She was trembling. *Her plan had failed!* she cried to herself. Taking deep gulps of air, she told herself over and over to calm down.

It had only been a business meeting—one that hadn't turned out as she'd hoped. Joe Lombardi had been as nice as could have been expected under the circumstances. After all, he'd had no prior warning of her offer. Was that an omen? she wondered. Would any man take her seriously?

She leaned her head back and closed her eyes, willing tense muscles to relax before she went any farther. She still had an hour's drive to Hooks Airport, just north of Houston, where she'd take the LaCroix private airplane back to Baton Rouge, Louisiana—in defeat.

It was just as well that Joe Lombardi hadn't accepted her offer. His type frightened her. He was one large package of raw, blatant masculinity. Handsome in a craggy, rugged way, he could probably get any woman he wanted. And once he had her, he probably knew exactly what to do with her. Visions of him tangled in soft, percale sheets had Sable's heartbeat quickening.

She opened her eyes and sat up straight. Joseph Lombardi was nothing like John. John had been soft and sweet and tender and understanding. He'd been vulnerable to others' opinions, yet excited about life, not touched by the world-weary attitude many men exhibited.

He had been everything that the man she'd just left wasn't. John could never have been tough. Rough. Raw-edged.

She still missed John's sage advice, his strong, quiet ways. She missed having someone to talk to.

John would never have grabbed a beer and glugged it down from a can.

For a moment she gave in to the tears that pressed on her lids. Two and a half years had only begun to heal her pain over the loss of the man who had been friend and brother and lover to her. Because of him she'd grown up and taken charge. She'd been the strong one; he'd been the wise one.

Again her thoughts returned to Joe. Strange that two such diverse individuals had been friends. War did exceptional things to otherwise ordinary mortals.

Enough of Joe Lombardi! It was time to work on an alternate plan. Somewhere out there was a suitable man who would be willing to marry her for a million dollars. She just had to find him.

Sable ignored the panic that was never far away. She had to find him fast. According to the LaCroix's attorney's secretary, John's parents would file custody papers soon. Over the past two years they had become fed up with Sable's restrictions, allowing Jonathan to visit them for no longer than a day instead of the weeks and months they'd at first requested, then demanded.

The LaCroix didn't know she had overhead them discussing their plans with the family attorney, or that his secretary was also her good friend. She knew she might not win in court. Louisiana still had its share of less than upright citizens in politics. Those who lived by whom, rather than what they knew, could still rule the courts. And her in-laws had influence like that.

No. She couldn't let the suit get to court. There were too many arguments against her case and in favor of the LaCroix.

Marriage, especially to someone living out of state, was her ace in the hole. But having lived a cloistered life since John's death, she knew of no eligible bachelors strong enough not to cave in to her in-laws. If she hadn't been cleaning out John's papers three weeks ago, she wouldn't even have remembered about Joe.

She had another week or so before the LaCroix filed their custody papers. She had to work fast. . . .

"Dammit!" she cried, hitting the steering wheel with her fist. It hurt, overriding the pain deep within her. "Why couldn't you have agreed, Mr. Beer-Drinking Lombardi? Who are you to laugh in my face? If you had agreed, everything would have been so easy. . . ."

Easy? She laughed aloud through her tears. Perhaps it was better this way. Joseph Lombardi was a reminder that she had limited experience with men. She might have been able to housebreak a kitten like John, but never a wildcat like Joe.

JOE HAD WORKED UP a great case of justifiable anger against his friend and attorney by the time Mike arrived.

"Why the hell didn't you just spit it out when you were here two days ago?" Leather-gloved hands on his hips, Joe stood beside Mike's car. "I felt like a damned fool, listening to John's widow explain in simple terms why she wanted to marry me!"

"Now, Joe," Mike began, stepping out of the small, red sportster. "I didn't realize she would follow through this quickly. That's all." He glanced warily at his client. "She's a good-looker, I hear."

Joe glared back. "She's a good-looker with a problem I don't need. What the hell possessed you to even consider such an offer for me? You're my attorney. Why didn't you tell her attorney to go to hell?"

"Because I thought you ought to hear her out. You need money immediately, and the bank's not willing to offer you another loan. Your new barn brought your credit limit to an end. You're overextended, Joe, and we both know it. Even though you have a racetrack license, you don't have the money or the backers to go forward with your own horses. If you had time, it'd be different. But you don't. When the state commission finds that your credit has run out, your license will be yanked. Quick."

Joe rubbed a gloved hand on the back of his neck. It was another hot day. Texas was filled with them. "If we had a few more weeks, I know we'd find some out-of-state backers."

"You'd have all the money you want and more if you took Sable LaCroix up on her offer."

Joe's eyes narrowed. "What do you know about her?"

Mike shrugged. "You knew her husband. That should be worth something."

"I don't know *her*. What do you know?" Joe repeated, his frustration barely held in check.

"That she's telling the truth. The LaCroix family wants its own. They're angry with her for taking their only grandson and moving away from the family home in New Orleans and into a house in Baton Rouge, out of range of their influence. Her husband was an only son who never quite made it out of their sphere. Now they want to raise their grandchild the same way."

Why was he listening to this? Marriage to anyone was out of the question, let alone this marriage to this woman! "And her?"

"Born and gently bred in Mobile, Alabama. She and a baby sister were raised by a widowed aunt, who'd never had children of her own. The aunt died about a year ago. When Sable met John, it was apparently love at first sight. He swept her off her feet. They were married three months after they met, and moved in with his parents. It was John's second marriage. His first wife died."

"I remember," Joe said slowly. Over the years Joe and John hadn't seen each other much, though they had exchanged occasional letters and Christmas cards, but finally even that small connection had faded.

A loud, male voice called his name. He muttered an oath and turned toward the sound. Two of his stallions were getting too close. Some fool had put them in adjoining paddocks.

"Look," Mike said quickly, pushing a file toward him. "Take a look at this and think on it. You don't have to make a decision right away. Just think about it."

Joe's head swiveled quickly. "Are you crazy?"

"No. I'm just trying to find a solution to your problem. I believe this is it."

Loud voices from the paddock area called again. Before Joe realized what was happening, his attorney was in his car, waving as he drove off.

Joe looked at the file in his hand, angry with himself for being unable to take care of two things at one time.

"Son of a . . ." he cursed, sticking the folder inside his blue plaid, flannel shirt. He'd go through the papers later. Right now he needed to chew somebody's butt for the trouble in the paddock.

TALIA WATCHED her sister park the rental car along the edge of the airstrip and slip the keys into the glove compartment, then walk toward the plane and its occupants, who were eagerly awaiting news of Mr. Lombardi's decision. She crossed her fingers. Talia prayed Sable's expression didn't reflect what had happened between herself and the man she'd picked to be her husband.

Once Sable appeared in the doorway of the private plane, Talia couldn't keep quiet any longer.

"Well? Did it go okay?" She continued to sit on the plushly carpeted floor, a child's plastic block in her hand. Her fingers clutched it like a talisman.

Little Johnny, his eyes brightening, stood up and ran toward her. "Mommy! Mommy!" he cried as he was swept into Sable's arms. His hug brought tears to her eyes. A lump formed in Talia's throat as she watched. No one, especially someone as sweet and vulnerable as her older sister, should have to fight so hard for what was hers. And Jonathan was hers.

"He said no," Sable announced over the youngster's shoulder. She looked as if she was using every ounce of control to remain calm.

"Damn!"

"Don't swear," Sable admonished, giving her son a kiss on his pudgy cheek. "Hello, dumpling."

"Sorry," Talia mumbled, standing up and sweeping imaginary lint from her jeans. She pushed her hair out of her eyes and glared. "Did he give a reason or just laugh in your face?"

"Both. He doesn't want to be married and he has no use for a child—or my money." Johnny squirmed, and she set him down, so he could run to a toy that had caught his interest.

Toys littered the roomy interior. The LaCroix family plane revealed how prepared her in-laws were to take custody of Johnny. All the boy's needs were kept on board, as they were at the three LaCroix homes.

Automatically Talia began rounding up the toys, preparing for takeoff.

"I'll do that," Sable said, reaching for the rest of the blocks and placing them in the playbox.

"Never mind," Talia told her, grabbing the toys randomly and throwing them into the lidded boxes. "Just tell me what we're going to do next."

"I don't know."

"Did you tell him about me? Did I jinx the deal?" Talia tried not to let her fear show in her voice, but she knew by her sister's expression that she'd failed.

Sable smiled reassuringly. "I didn't even get to you, honey. He cut me off at the pass."

"Well, it's his loss," Talia declared defensively. "How could the man be so stupid? If he was a friend of John's, he had to have *some* intelligence."

"It doesn't matter. It's our loss, too," Sable pointed out softly.

The pilot came on board. "Are we ready, Mrs. LaCroix?"

"Ready." Sable stood and placed her son in the seat next to hers, then strapped both of them in, while Talia did the same across from them.

"We'll be in the air in just a minute. Baton Rouge in an hour and a half, ma'am."

"Thank you," Sable said tiredly, and Talia's heart went out to her. People always assumed Sable was strong, because she shouldered so much responsibility, but Talia knew how hard it was for her. Sometimes Talia felt older than her sister, as if she were nine years the senior.

The pilot disappeared into the cockpit, and she sat back and closed her eyes, listening to Johnny bubble in delight at the pictures of the hard-paged book in Sable's lap.

Thanks to Joe Lombardi's decision, it looked as if the war was over, and they hadn't even fought one battle.

Just then Sable looked over at her. "Don't worry, Spike," she said over the roar of the engines. "The fight isn't over. Not yet."

Talia grinned at her childhood nickname. "You bet." She wondered what she could do to ease the pain she saw in her sister's eyes, but nothing came to mind.

Sable's marriage to an older man had been perfect for her. It had allowed her to grow and learn what her capabilities were. Normally a homebody, Sable had found she was an efficient hostess and party-goer when the need arose. But she was happiest caring for babies and cooking and keeping the neatest house on the block. All the things that Talia hated.

Talia had always gotten whatever she went after. Why couldn't Sable have what she wanted? It didn't seem fair. Suddenly things weren't black and white anymore, but blending shades of gray.

At seventeen she was beginning to realize just how complicated life could be. She hoped it wasn't a permanent affliction. She liked thing simple and straightforward.

JOE RAN THE FIGURES through the calculator again, then compared them to the computer tape printout. They matched. He had hoped they wouldn't.

Mike was right. If he didn't raise half a million dollars within the week, he'd lose the chance of a lifetime. Only three racetracks were to be built in Texas. The other two were corporate enterprises, and his was the only private one. He knew of at least seven other men who could quickly take his place, once the racing commission found out his letter of credit had been withdrawn.

Sable's million dollars was the answer. It dangled in front of him like bait before a hungry bass. He tried to ignore the vision, but the offer was tantalizing.

Ahab, his prized thoroughbred, hadn't won enough races yet to be considered worth a million dollars. Not to a banker, who needed more reassurance than his trainer Totty's word. If Ahab won the next two big ones, however, Joe might be able to claim he was worth that much. But by that time it would be too late....

With Sable LaCroix's million he could *immediately* obtain a letter for another million and open the track on time.

He had no choice—not if he didn't want to lose control of the entire operation by bringing in corporate investors, who would also be major stockholders.

He needed Sable LaCroix's money.

What he didn't need was her problems.

He didn't have a choice.

Before he changed his mind, he reached for the phone and dialed Mike's number.

His words were to the point. "Mike, tell Sable LaCroix the deal is on. I need the money in my account within the week."

"When do you want to get married?"

"How do I know? That's her problem. Tell her to make all the arrangements, and I'll be there." He tapped his pencil against the desk calendar. "One more thing. She has to live here. I expect her to be a wife, not a flittering social butterfly. I also want a prenuptial agreement. When the marriage is over, we each go our separate ways with no financial attachment to the other. Is that clear?"

"Perfectly," Mike said dryly. "Do you want me to draw up the divorce papers while I write out the prenuptial agreement?"

"Why not? I doubt she'll last a year, if that long. This isn't exactly heaven for a female out here. Especially not her kind. The grocery store is over twenty miles away, to say nothing of the nearest boutique."

"I'll call her," Mike promised him. "But I can't guarantee she'll buy all your provisions."

"She will." Joe knew he sounded far more confident than he felt.

It was done. He didn't dare look too closely at why he had agreed to the marriage. Financial need was a good enough excuse for what he was doing. He refused to admit to any other reason.

SABLE HUNG UP the phone and tapped her pencil against the desk calendar. Hope blossomed in her breast. She smiled.

He had agreed!

The prenuptial agreement was fine with her. She had to protect Johnny's future. If Joe hadn't mentioned it, she would have brought it up herself.

With the exception of the million dollars needed to buy the groom, her money would remain hers, and his money would remain his. She had also stipulated separate bedrooms, and her attorney and Mike, Joe's attorney, would draw up a marriage contract. They were to remain together, at Joe's home, for a minimum of five years, with neither having lovers nor affairs, or the agreement would be dissolved. If Joe broke the agreement, Sable's money had to be returned within ninety days. At the end of the contract they could divorce, as Sable believed by then the LaCroix would no longer be interested in gaining custody of her son.

Sable would have no problem keeping to the terms of their deal. She hoped Joe wouldn't, either.

The wedding arrangements were left to her.

She studied the calendar. In one week she would be married and living out of state. The LaCroix family might have influence in Louisiana, but their influence didn't reach as far as Texas. Let them try to prove her an unfit mother, when she was the wife of a man whose name was as well-known in Texas as their son's in Louisiana. She had just bought her guarantee that Johnny was hers.

Talia stuck her head around the door. "Everything okay?"

"Better than okay. How would you like to be a bridesmaid?"

Sable saw her little sister's eyes widen. "Who bought it?"

"Joe Lombardi."

If it was possible, Talia's eyes opened even wider. "Really?" she squeaked, bouncing into the room and perching on the side of the desk. "When?"

"Next week."

Talia frowned. "Have you told him about me being part of the package deal?"

"Not yet. I'll tell him when the time is right."

"You don't think I'll jinx the deal, do you?"

Sable's hand covered her sister's. "Not a chance. He's marrying me because he needs the money. I'm marrying him because we need a protector. We both get what we want. It's a simple business deal."

Talia glanced down, then back up at her sister, her brown eyes showing her vulnerability. "Does he know why you won't fight for Johnny in court?"

Leaning back, Sable stared at the hand that lay on top of her sister's. They were still together. "The custody suit you and I went through has nothing to do with him. It's none of his concern."

Talia looked at her—wise beyond her years, Sable reflected. "Regardless of the fact that you were the one our parents fought over?"

"That's not true and you know it. Dad fought for me because I was easier to care for, that's all."

"Honest?"

Sable smiled. It was the truth as she saw it. They had never really discussed it, although both had thought about it plenty. Talia had gone through hell in those days. She still bore the emotional scars inflicted by parents who hadn't been mature enough to behave like adults. But with lots of love Talia had pulled through— no thanks to their parents. Sable would not let Jonathan go through the same pain.

"Honest."

Talia's expression eased. She sat down in the red leather wing chair and leaned forward. "Good. Now, business or not, this is a wedding. What are you going to wear?"

2

SABLE PACED her study for a full hour before she finally found the nerve to dial Joe's number. She found him intimidating and highly frustrating, so she had put off their conversation until there were too many unanswered questions to be ignored. For three days she had not only been planning a wedding, but also a change of residence for herself and two others. And Joe Lombardi had never called her.

She let the phone ring—seven, eight, nine times. She was afraid that if she hung up she'd never have enough nerve to try again. Besides, it was better to try to reach him while she was still angry with the LaCroix's latest move. They had just informed her that they wanted Johnny to remain in Louisiana whenever she used the company plane. They were still ignorant of her wedding plans, and she wanted to keep things that way until the last moment but she still worried that they might suspect.

On the eleventh ring the phone was picked up. "Tejas Stables," Joe barked into the receiver.

If his tone was any indication of his mood, this phone call was going to require all her strength and tact.

"Mr. Lombardi?" she questioned hesitantly, praying it was someone else.

"Yes, what is it?"

This was going to be harder than she thought. "This is Sable LaCroix. I need some questions answered. Are you free for a few minutes?"

"Right now?"

"Yes." Her answer was firm. Her knees were weak.

A heavy sigh filled the wires. "I've got exactly five minutes, honey. Ahab's getting loaded onto a truck, so Totty can drive him to a race in Louisiana. Start asking."

Honey? He had some nerve! Sable wished she had time to count to ten. And who in the world was Totty? Instead she plunged ahead. "Is the entire house furnished?"

Silence.

She tried again. "How many bedrooms are there?"

Silence.

"How many baths?"

A sigh.

Now she was getting somewhere, she just wasn't sure where. "Do you have a washer and dryer?"

A groan, but still no answer.

"How large is the garage? Are there shelves for books? Is there enough storage area or should I rent a space? Is there a dishwasher?"

She stopped for a breath and waited.

Still no answer.

"Mr. Lombardi? Are you there?"

His voice was low, sounding tired. "Honey, I think you should come here and look around. I've lived here over five years, and I never thought of noticing half of what you're asking. It's not important for me to know. But if it is to you, then pick a time when I'm gone all day, and you can answer your questions to your heart's content."

"I don't have time, Mr. Lombardi," she stated firmly. "I'm trying to do most of the plans for the wedding from here, so I won't lose time packing. But I need answers, so I know what to pack and what to discard."

"Just pack a suitcase—one for you, one for the kid—and get your rump to Texas. You can handle the rest from here. Anything that doesn't go in a suitcase, you don't need."

He knew better than to make stupid statements like that, and this man wasn't stupid, so he was having fun by harassing her. It wasn't going to work. She wouldn't be put off.

Ignoring his comments, Sable plunged ahead. "As for the wedding, Mr. Lombardi, it's being held in your living room. I have a right to have my things around me, as much as you have a right to have yours. I'm only trying to work out a compromise in the easiest way possible."

"Then come and look around before moving in. I don't have time to answer questions. I've got a racetrack to build."

Her anger rose in response to his rudeness. "May I remind you that without answers to these questions, I might not marry you," she told him coldly. "Then you wouldn't have the necessary money to complete your pet project."

"Suit yourself, honey. I can always find other backers, but I still have to get the racetrack ready."

She tapped her nails on the edge of the rosewood desk. He was calling her bluff. She didn't know how much truth there was in his last sentence—and didn't have the nerve to find out.

"All right, Mr. Lombardi," she said reluctantly, resigning herself to the inevitable. "I'll be there in two days."

"Fine," he answered. "The front door's always open. Just walk in and make yourself at home."

"Thank you," she said stiffly. "I will."

"Don't I know it," he muttered before hanging up. Sable was left with a dial tone in her ear and a thousand curses in five languages on the tip of her tongue.

She had two days to count to ten—five thousand times. Maybe then, and only then, she could control her temper enough not to lose it within the next three minutes of conversation with Mr. Joe Lombardi!

JOE JUMPED into the truck, gunned the engine and sped out of the yard toward the dirt road leading to the track.

He felt ashamed of the way he'd just acted toward Sable, and shame always made him act overly tough and aggressive.

Couldn't she understand? His prize thoroughbred was on his way to a sweepstakes race. He was in the middle of building a racetrack, with the Texas government breathing down his neck. And she was asking about dishwashers!

She needed to get her priorities straight!

Wasn't he helping her out enough by marrying her?

The dirt swirled around the fast-moving truck as his thoughts raced further ahead. He needed money, and she needed a respectable husband.

Well, he could live with that. What he didn't need was a wife, helpmate and leech, who would want his time and whine over his every move. He'd been single too long for that nonsense.

There had always been women when he'd needed them. Today's women only asked for equal treatment and a good time. He gave them both. Then, with neither guilt nor regret, he moved on to the next one.

But Sable LaCroix wasn't that kind of woman. He doubted if she knew what bra burning was all about. She was a throwback to gentler, Southern ways. And so their conversation had been rougher than normal, because he was trying to make a point. He was his own man, and she wasn't going to change his life-style. Period.

He hoped she'd gotten the message.

TWO DAYS LATER, Sable drove her station wagon over the Montgomery County line in Texas with a smile of satisfaction.

Joe Lombardi had told her to answer her own questions—and she would do just that. Instead of one suitcase, however, she had a matched set of six, a box of toys for Johnny and five cases of books. The moving company would bring the rest.

She turned onto a farm-to-market road, an antiquated Texas term left over from the times when farms surrounded the cities, and counties built just a few good roads for farmers to travel with their produce. This one led to Joe's place.

Sable had a feeling that Joe enjoyed his bachelor freedom too much to give it up lightly. He probably

thought threats and rough talk would make clear his
intention to be boss in their marriage. He didn't know
her very well. In fact he didn't know her at all. Obviously no one had told him that hens usually ruled the
roost, and that the rooster was there only on suffer-
ance.

But when it came to her son, Sable was a tigress.
She'd do anything to keep Johnny. Anything—including marrying a bully of a man. And if the man didn't
like it—tough luck. According to his attorney, he'd already agreed to her terms. Besides, whom was he fooling when he said he could find backers? If that had been
the case, he wouldn't have agreed to this marriage in the
first place.

After thinking through his threats, Sable had realized that Joe Lombardi had as little choice as she did.
And that kept her smiling.

After following a dirt lane about half a mile off the
main thoroughfare, she pulled up in front of Joe's
house. It was a big, rambling ranch house that looked
as if each owner had built an addition to it with no re-
gard for an overall, architectural design. However, despite having wings and windows placed at odd angles,
it all came together very well, reminding Sable of an old
grande dame who still wore feathers and pearls with her
silk dresses and high-buttoned shoes. A unique style,
it was unacceptable on anyone else. On this old lady it
was perfect.

She pulled up to the porch that ran the length of the
front and one side and stepped out. Paint had bubbled
and flaked away around the eaves. The porch floor, although sturdy, also needed a new coat of paint.

She opened the screen door to find the front door wide open, as Joe had said it would be. Joe was either trusting or foolhardy to leave his home unlocked this close to a huge metropolis like Houston.

But as she wandered through the rooms, she began to see that the only damage an interloper could do here would be to spray-paint the walls—and considering their condition, that just might be an improvement.

The living-room furniture was in colonial style and at least twenty years old. Sable lifted a couch cushion and wrinkled her nose. Hard-candy wrappers and bottle tops were scattered here and there, along with crumbs of what looked like potato chips. She'd bet the furniture had never been cleaned.

The dining-room set was solid mahogany. This she knew only because she wiped off at least ten years of dust to find the grain and color. The china cabinet held beautiful, floral-patterned dishes and cut crystal water and wineglasses, along with sterling silver serving pieces. Or rather she thought they were silver beneath the tarnish.

All four bedrooms were furnished with plain, sturdy pieces. But nothing matched. The spreads and curtains were in keeping with the furniture—nothing matched there, either.

Mr. Joseph Lombardi was consistent in his taste: he had none.

The kitchen, however, was the masterpiece. Dishes were stacked on one side of the sink, while the other side was clean and clear. The sink itself was filled with pots and pans soaking in sudsy, cold water. She peeked into the dishwasher. It was spotlessly clean and empty. Joe Lombardi obviously didn't use this appliance.

The blue-gray Formica table was spotless, but the floor was a mess. The tile could have been either gray or white, Sable couldn't tell. Now it was a spotted tan with dirty-brown boot marks in strategic places, like the doorway and in front of the refrigerator and sink.

Just off the kitchen she could see a utility room with a washer, dryer and a set-up ironing board piled high with clothing, as well as an upright freezer.

Carefully Sable opened the refrigerator and peeked inside. She found ketchup, mustard, relish, mild and piquant sauces and milk. Two open containers of luncheon meat and cheese completed the food list. The rest of the space on the shelves was filled with at least three twelve-packs of beer.

She wrinkled her nose in distaste. "Mr. Lombardi, you're in for quite a culture shock," she announced, firmly shutting the door.

Sable retraced her steps to the front of the house and descended the steps to unload the car.

Half an hour later as she reached for the last box, she spied dirt swirling on the road to the house. "The cavalry, no doubt," she panted, carefully balancing the box as she headed up the porch steps once more. "And just in the nick of time . . . for one of us."

Before the truck pulled to a halt in the driveway, she managed to open the screen door and make it down the hallway to the bedroom she'd declared her own. All she had to do was inform the master of the house—after she'd moved in.

Wiping suddenly damp hands on the back of her slacks, she walked back and casually leaned against the doorjamb while Joe came toward the house. She tried for a condescending smile. Better to let him know now how it was between them than to find out later she hadn't written the right guidelines.

She felt his gaze dissolve every piece of clothing from her body. His eyes told her he appreciated what, but not necessarily whom he saw.

He was raw virility.

His blue plaid shirt brought out his golden tan and the matching blue of his eyes. His broad chest and muscled arms strained against the fabric.

He was as handsome as sin.

"Hello, *sweetie*. I didn't expect you to be waiting at the door for me," he said as he strode up the steps, only to stop within inches of her. "But these days it's not enough just to be decorative. Next time have an open beer in your hand."

And he was quite obnoxious.

"Look closely, *sweetlings*," she said stiffly. "Because you'll never see me in this domestic-bliss position again, let alone with a beer in my hand."

His brows rose, but a smile still lurked at the corners of his mouth. A very male, very smug smile. "Are we upset about something, *darlingkins*?"

"Nothing in particular, *honey bun*, except that you choose to live in squalor and I won't."

Now his voice held an edge. "Then clean it, *sweetlings*."

"No way, *darling*. It's not *my* dirt. It's yours."

Joe's chest expanded as he took a deep, exasperated breath. "Dirt is dirt. I don't pander to helpless little females, so if you want a clean home, clean it yourself."

Sable stood even straighter, her eyes blazing. "I am a very good housekeeper. Probably the best you've ever known. But I will *not* clean years of accumulated dirt that I had nothing to do with. Nor will I live in it."

Joe cocked his head. "So what do you plan to do about it, brown eyes?"

She smiled, and for just a fleeting second she saw the fear her reaction gave Joe. "I expect you to have a cleaning crew in here within the next three days to scrub this place from top to bottom. If they don't, then we can call the whole deal off."

He believed she'd do it! "Just like that?"

Sable nodded, her gaze steel-hard. "Just like that."

His eyes narrowed. "And what other conditions do you have up your sleeve?"

"That's it, Mr. Lombardi. I will keep *our* house clean from the wedding on. But I refuse to clean your old mess for you."

A war was raging inside him, she could tell. Sable held her breath. She had no idea if he would remain obstinate, but this first confrontation would tell what kind of man he was. She crossed her fingers behind her back and waited.

"Okay. I agree," he finally muttered. "It isn't fair for you to clean what isn't your dirt. I'll have a crew in here immediately."

She let her breath out slowly and smiled. Joe took a step back, then swung around and went inside the house. But just as she turned to follow, pleased with his answer, he ruined it all.

"But mind you," Joe threw over his shoulder as he walked to the kitchen and opened the refrigerator door. "I expect you to keep this place spotless after that. You're home all day with nothing to do."

"Nothing to do?" she repeated softly. "Nothing to do?" she practically shouted. "I happen to have a son who is in the middle of his messy period. And for the past two years I've been chairman of several charities, to say nothing of my foundation to help the hungry children in America!"

Joe popped the top of his can and took a long, thirsty pull. Wiping his mouth on his shirt sleeve he grinned. "La-di-da, soon-to-be Mrs. Lombardi. Your charities are in Louisiana, not here. My wife will drop those things that have nothing to do with this state."

Her next words dripped poison. "You mean like invest in a beer distributorship? Or find great locations to drop off the weekly barn-mucking offal? Or perhaps I could volunteer at shelters for the battered and neglected wives of racehorse owners."

His face was a thundercloud, his tone a soft warning. "Don't push, Sable. This whole situation is hard enough already."

It was obviously time to try a different tack. "You're right," she said, her eyes demurely downcast. "There's no sense arguing right now. We can work it out later. Together."

His eyes narrowed as he stared at her. She gazed back, her expression bland. *Let him make what he wants of it*, she thought, she wasn't going to queer the deal now. Not when he'd agreed to hire a cleaning crew. Sable had an idea that when it came to women, most of him was bluff and the rest indecision. She'd have plenty of time to test out her theory later.

"By the way," she asked softly. "Do you mind if I take the bedroom across the hall from yours? It's the perfect size, and there's a connecting door to what will be Johnny's room. That way, if he's restless, you won't lose sleep. I can be with him in an instant."

"Be my guest," he replied, though his expression was anything but gracious.

"Thank you." She smiled sweetly.

Joe let out a grunt of exasperation. "What are your plans for moving in?"

"I'm returning home tonight to pack the rest of my things." She gave him a coy glance through her lashes. "You don't mind if I have the moving company bring a few pieces of my furniture, do you? Jonathan needs his own bedroom set, and of course I have my own, too."

"Anything else?" he asked dryly.

She knew her act wasn't fooling him, but she went through with it, anyway. "Oh, there's a few pieces of furniture I'd like to add to yours, if it's all right. I promise it will only enhance the rooms, not crowd them."

"Now listen carefully," he admonished, his face stern. "I don't want my life-style changed. I like my furniture. I like the way it looks. It's neat, and there's no fussy gewgaws around to collect dust or get broken."

"Really? Early bachelor decor appeals to you, does it?"

"Yes." He bit the word out.

"Well, a little more style appeals to me," she told him, barely containing her temper. "And there doesn't appear to be a drop of it in this house."

"Fine. Just keep it confined to your bedroom."

She tilted her chin. "If that's the way you want it."

"I do."

Sable turned on her heel and marched down the hall to "her" bedroom, slamming the door behind her.

Leaning against the cool wood, she breathed deeply, trying to calm her pounding heart. Damn that man! He gave orders like a king! Giving orders as if he owned the place!

He does own the place, her too logical mind answered.

Her temper dissolved. She felt a smile quirk the corners of her mouth. The smile turned into a giggle, which grew into laughter.

JOE STOOD at the kitchen window, taking several deep, cleansing breaths. Blood pounded in his ears, and he wasn't sure if it was due to anger or arousal. Either way his reaction was the same.

Sable had a way of getting under his skin and scrambling his thoughts, until he didn't know what he was saying anymore! Her sparkling, brown eyes, her light, flowery scent twisted his tongue and made him sound like a schoolboy. The sight of her long-limbed body encased in expensive, clinging slacks and a sweater that probably cost as much as his feed bill drove him up the wall.

So here he stood. They'd just had an argument, and she'd had the audacity to walk away from him into "her" room. He wanted her back in the kitchen. *His* kitchen! The whole house was his!

What was the matter with her? Hadn't he just graciously given in and said she didn't have to clean the house? Hadn't he said he'd get a cleaning crew in here, pronto? Was it too much to ask that she keep it clean from then on? Or was she too spoiled to see the leeway he'd willingly given her?

No, that wasn't quite true. He'd been riding her ever since that last phone call, and they both knew it. He had purposely used harsh words and curt actions to keep distance between them. Obviously it wasn't working, or he'd be in better shape than he was right now. The symptoms were more than apparent: he was in his cavemanlike, kiss-her-or-kill-her mode. But he was a civilized man and would wait for the feelings to subside. Confusion always made him feel aggressive.

He admitted, at least to himself, that he didn't know much about the workings of a woman's mind. He'd never had time or inclination to study them. On a one-to-one basis he'd always found they were either nice or they weren't. That was all he needed to know, or so he'd thought until now. Suddenly he wished he understood those small nuances that some men seemed to have a knack of picking up. He was lost.

A sigh left his lips and anger drained with the breath. He wasn't scared of Sable LaCroix. He was scared to death of his reaction to her. And he was even more afraid to let her know. This was a business proposition. She'd made that fact clear from the beginning. The least he could do was to remember that. Then he wouldn't find himself making a pass, only to be turned down and embarrassed.

A sound—faint at first—filtered down the hallway to the kitchen. As it became louder he recognized it. Sable was laughing. Laughing! Behind his closed door and while he was frustrated and in pain, Sable was laughing!

He didn't know how he got to "her" bedroom door, but his hand had turned the knob even before he realized he was there. He pushed against it, and with little resistance it opened.

"Something funny?" Joe's tone was acerbic as he stared into her twinkling, brown eyes.

"Yes," she gurgled, still barely able to keep the laughter under control. "I was laughing at myself. I was so angry at you for acting as if you owned this house. Then I realized that you did. Own it, I mean."

"And that's funny?"

She nodded, her brown hair catching the last rays of the afternoon sun. "Don't you think so?"

His mouth quirked against his wishes. "Yeah," he finally admitted. "I guess so."

Sable giggled again, and the sound sped sensuously down his spine. "I'm surprised that I didn't order you out of your own house," she chortled. "Can you imagine?"

He couldn't hold his smile in check any longer. "And I'd have reminded you whose house it was."

"And left me speechless and totally without dignity!"

He glanced down her enticing figure, then back up to her eyes. She was desirable. And absolutely beautiful. "This is dignity?" he asked, knowing it was either tease her or kiss her.

"This is as good a try at dignity as I'm going to get under the circumstances," she teased back. "At least I'm trying."

Sable took a deep breath to control her laughter. He was sure she didn't realize what she did to him when she placed her slender hand against his chest. "I'm sorry," she said. "It's just so darn funny."

"Sable LaCroix, you're something else." Joe took a step closer to her, leaving barely an inch of space between them. "Something very unusual."

Her smile drifted away as she stared into his eyes. He hoped he wasn't reading her reaction wrong, because he was going to kiss her, no matter what.

"Really?" she asked. Her voice was soft, wispy, and he was drowning in her big, brown eyes.

"Really," he growled, just before covering her lips with his. Her mouth was soft, her breath as warm as a summer day. And he absorbed it until he could feel the freshness of her down to his toes.

His tongue asked for admittance and she acquiesced. She wrapped her arms around his neck as he pulled her closer and deepened the kiss, feeling her body flow against his in molten delight. How had he gone so long without knowing this wonderful feeling? he wondered. Then his mind went blank as pleasure took over.

Somewhere in the distance a car backfired, and with the sound reality returned.

Joe eased away.

Sable was startled to find herself feeling bereft. It was a struggle to open her eyes and stare up at him. She wanted to feel him, not see him.

"Are you all right?" His voice was as rough as coarse sandpaper.

She nodded, then cleared her throat. "I'm fine." What a stupid thing to say! She was not fine! She was fraying at the edges from a kiss that had robbed her of all sense!

"We shouldn't have done that."

She shook her head. "No, you shouldn't. This is a business deal. Nothing more." Her insides still quaked from his touch. *It was just a kiss!* she told herself, still stunned by the strength of her reaction.

"On the other hand," he continued, ignoring her gentle rebuke. "Maybe it's good we got this out of the way now. We would have always wondered what it would be like to kiss. Now we know."

Sable stared blankly at him. "Now we know what?"

His lips turned up in a smile, displaying a deep dimple just below one eye. His finger traced the outline of her lips before he answered, and she found herself pouting in reaction to his touch. "Now we know what it's like to kiss. Our curiosity is abated."

"Right," she murmured, her mind still dazed. "Our curiosity is abated."

"Now we can get on with this business arrangement and not let our, uh, personal observations get in the way."

Sable finally took his point. "Your curiosity is abated. Mine was never piqued."

His husky chuckle filled the air. "You make one hell of a lousy liar, Sable. But if that's what it takes for you to feel better about yourself . . ."

Her backbone stiffened, as if all the vertebrae had suddenly been glued together. "No lies, Mr. Lombardi. Just the plain and simple truth. It never occurred to me to make your kisses a fantasy of mine. Your kiss was nice, but please don't worry about my panting to repeat it. It was just another kiss. That's all."

Joe's smile disappeared and a frown creased his forehead. "Right," he snapped. "Now what are those boxes doing in the corner?"

She followed his gaze. "Those boxes are books and Johnny's toys. Since I had to come here, I brought them to save moving time."

"Do you have your answers now?"

"Yes."

"Good. Don't bother telling me what you found out. I'm not interested. You can go on your way, and I can get back to work before I lose the entire day fooling around."

"If you 'fool around,' as you so aptly put it, then it's not my fault. I got my answers on my own, unpacked on my own, and now I'm leaving. On my own."

"Then we don't have a problem, do we?" he practically shouted.

"No problem at all," she answered in kind.

After a hard, blue-eyed stare, he left her. His steps echoed down the hallway to the front door. The screen squeaked open, then closed with a resounding bang.

Sable held her head in her hands and prayed for control. She had more problems than she could shake a

stick at, and all of them had to do with her husband-
to-be, Joe Lombardi.

JOE SLID into the front seat and fired up the truck, gun-
ning the engine as soon as it started.

No problem, he'd said. Whom was he kidding? He
had more problems than he could cope with! For two
cents he'd call the whole thing off. But for a million he'd
try to make the best of it. All he had to do was remember that Sable LaCroix was more of a problem than he
could handle, and that would remind him to keep his
distance.

Somehow the idea of keeping his distance wasn't as
reassuring as it should have been.

3

IT TOOK the cleaning crew three days. They cleaned in places Joe didn't even know existed and some he didn't want to know about at all. They even went through his personal closet, then straightened out the linen closet, which had become a catchall over the years for anything made of fabric, including the mending.

He had to admit that Sable was right. The place had only been surface-cleaned in the past, and years of dust and dirt had made their way throughout the house. After the carpeting was steam-cleaned he realized the rug was rust-colored, not brown.

And much as he hated to admit it, Joe liked the "new" look.

What he didn't like was Sable pointing it out to him. Dammit, he'd been too busy earning a living to be a hausfrau, too! Besides, he was only home for morning and evening meals and to sleep. Almost all his free time was spent with the men in the bunkhouse, where they made plans for the next day's work or watched televised sports.

Now his life was changing. Sable was coming to live here, and no matter how hard he tried to pretend that things would remain the same, he knew they would not. Any woman was bound to upset his life. That the woman was Sable . . . he stopped his thoughts whenever they strayed to her.

After duly admiring their work, he paid off the cleaning crew and ushered them out. At last the house was quiet once more. He reached into the fridge for a beer and pulled the tab.

There was no sense in going back out to the track. It was almost quitting time for the men. Besides, he'd run from his thoughts ever since Sable had left. He needed to confront them and get himself back together before she returned at the end of the week.

He was marrying Sable LaCroix on Sunday afternoon.

He plopped onto the couch and stared out the front bay window at the towering pines that shielded his home from the farm road beyond. He lived in a forest that hid his personal paradise, giving him privacy to relax, away from the prying eyes of the civilized world.

He was almost there.

His life-style had reflected his goals: Keep Your Nose to the Grindstone—and look neither left nor right, unless you're changing lanes. He liked his life that way. It had been easier to know he had to plow forward rather than run in circles. Until now.

Ever since he'd left the service and moved to Conroe, where he'd worked on a thoroughbred ranch, he'd been knee-deep in plans and saving every dime he earned for his dream. Knowing he had a knack, an instinct with animals and the races they could win, he'd pursued that dream. He'd vowed he would have his ranch someday, and six years ago his dream had come true. He'd been happy from the moment he'd signed the papers to this place.

In those days he'd even attempted to clean it on a regular basis. Occasionally a female came over and fussed, showing how domesticated and necessary she was to him, but then she'd leave, and Joe would go back to his own ways. That had been before his horses won a few of the more important races and he learned the value of a good reputation to the world of finance. Nothing was more important than his career.

Thanks to Ahab's stud capabilities and the right combination of genes, he now had three blue-ribbon winners. They'd made him a millionaire. His dream had come true.

Having attained one goal, he began looking around for another.

Then last year the state of Texas had decided that horse racing—with betting—was a legitimate business. Everyone and his brother tried out for the licenses. Out of over three hundred entries, his and four others had passed muster. Three other horse breeders and Mike, his attorney, had formed a partnership. Then had begun the long process of completing the necessary paperwork.

The racing commission checked him over each step of the way, cross-examining him in public courts, testing the truth of each of his words by double-checking, and then making him cool his heels before they gave him the next set of red tape to work through. His friends had supplied the commission with glowing recommendations. His luck had held, and the racetrack was to be the only one in the fourteen surrounding counties.

Since the other investors were silent partners, to all intents and purposes this was *his* track, his baby. He had to channel all his efforts and energy into this demanding task, or fail.

Sable's million dollars meant that Joe retained the controlling interest; it would be used as collateral for another two million. He needed the loan desperately. The other investors were tapped out—broke—until they received a return on their investment. Just as broke as he was. Everything he had or ever would have was tied up in this deal. He wanted to own the best track in the state. In the country. Landscaping alone was costing half a million. He was sparing no expense, providing larger-than-theater seats, public and private lounges, and elaborate quarters for both horses and jockeys. Someday he'd have a national race at his track, one equal to the Preakness Stakes or the Kentucky Derby.

And in the midst of all these crises he was getting *married*.

Joe leaned his head back and closed his eyes. Maybe once all this wedding hoopla was over and they settled into some kind of routine, it wouldn't be so bad. After all, she had a child and a house to care for and shower attention on, while he went about, doing his own thing.

The memory of their kiss came back to haunt him. It was unlike all the other kisses he'd ever had, and he resented that. But while resentment built in his mind, his body had a whole different list of possibilities and reacted every time he thought of her. Even now his skin flushed, and he tingled all the way down to his knees. He wished she were here to repeat it . . . just to see if it was as good as his memory kept telling him.

Whom are you kidding, Lombardi? he demanded. *That kiss was as close to fire as you've ever gotten. Only intense fear made you end it. Fear of getting involved with a woman who could take you away from your goal. Repeat it and you might get burned so badly, you'd never recover!*

All his instincts told him to run from Sable as quickly and as far as he could. But he had to ignore those instincts. He had no choice in the matter. Not if he wanted to continue building his dream.

And the racetrack, he kept reminding himself, was what this whole charade was about. The track was his first love and the one that counted. The one he stood to lose, if he didn't continue to concentrate on it.

The thought stiffened his resolve. Right. He had no choice. From now on he'd be nice and kind—and keep his distance from Mrs. Sable LaCroix. That way they'd both be able to stick to their parts of the bargain. Otherwise, he was sure he'd live to regret it.

His fingers tightened on the barely touched beer can. Forcing his eyes open, he banished the image of Sable staring up at him, brown eyes sultry and half-closed. He'd wanted to ravish her there and then. He still did. But he was a grown man. He should be able to handle temptation by now. Especially considering what was at stake.

Sable was just a woman—and he was just a man. Two ordinary people. That was all. Just because they were man and woman didn't mean they had to play

Adam and Eve. Hell, he'd seen lots of beautiful women in his time and still hadn't gotten emotionally involved.

He sighed. "Get off your rear, Lombardi," he chided himself. "And finish the paperwork you've been putting off."

He proceeded to do just that.

SABLE STARED around her study. She would miss this small, but comfortable room. It held an antique lady's desk in Queen Anne style, two chairs, a filing cabinet and several small paintings she'd collected over the years. The colors were light: peach and green with sprays of white. It was a restful place, next to Jonathan's room, so she could listen for him in the evening. His room was also done in pastel colors, but its walls were hung with pictures of balloons and teddy bears.

She was excited, but there was also an overriding sorrow. By this time next week she would be Mrs. Joseph Lombardi. The end of one life and the beginning of another.

Married. She vaguely remembered feeling this way when she'd left her aunt's home to marry John. She'd been young and impressionable, scared and unbelievably excited, even though her aunt had at the best of times been what the kids now called a "downer," pouring cold water on everything fun.

Looking back, Sable had often wondered if she'd married John as much to get away from the older woman's influence as because she was in love with him. But she banished those thoughts immediately, because they smacked of treason to John's memory.

The truth was, she had met and fallen in love with him as a teenager of nineteen and married him the day after her twentieth birthday. She had admired him almost as a father figure because he was eleven years older. But over the first two years of their marriage their roles had slowly shifted. She'd become the mother, nurturing him as if she were taking up where his mother had left off. Now she wasn't sure how their marriage would have developed in later years.

When John died, Sable had never dreamed she'd marry again. He'd left her with a child she adored and more than enough money to keep her in style for the rest of her life. Every time she saw her financial statement, her inheritance staggered her. Ironically, it was John's money that had bought her new groom.

She'd thought she'd never have to marry again, because she had her own form of independence. Weren't money and love two of the main reasons most women married? Wasn't financial security the main reason for most second marriages?

Yet here she was, getting married again. Love had nothing to do with it. Money did.

Three years ago she'd been content, caring for her son and sister, and living with the sweetest and gentlest man she'd ever known. John. Now she was contemplating a life where she would be a wife in name only—and she was *paying* the man to agree to it!

The office door opened slightly, interrupting Sable's reverie. Her sister gazed through the widening crack. "Getting prenuptial jitters?" Talia asked.

When Sable chuckled, Talia knew it was okay to enter. She walked in and perched on the arm of the wing chair.

"Hardly," Sable stated dryly. She was unwilling to admit her feelings of confusion to anyone, even to Talia.

Talia studied Sable's expression. "Then why the frown?"

"There's just so much to do and such a short time to sort it all out." Sable tried to contain her sigh. She couldn't admit to jitters, but they'd plagued her ever since she'd overheard John's parents discussing how to obtain custody of Jonathan.

"Anything I can do to help?"

Sable smiled. "Not so far, but I'll keep you in mind for some of the bigger problems."

"Right," Talia drawled, knowing full well her sister wouldn't let her handle anything larger than an occasional frying pan. "Have you told your future husband about me yet?"

Sable shifted in her seat. "Not yet."

Talia stared. "Why not?"

"The subject just hasn't come up yet."

"Liar," her little sister declared. "You're chicken." Then Talia's eyes widened. "Are you afraid he'll say no to the deal if he finds out about me?"

"Not really," Sable hedged. "I just thought it'd be easier to present you as a fait accompli."

"What's that?"

"It means that it's already done."

"*After* the wedding?"

Sable nodded, hoping her sister wouldn't feel too bad about being kept a secret.

"You really think that's wise?"

"There are so many other things to worry about right now. I can't see where telling him later will do any harm."

Talia furrowed her brow as she worried through the information. She was far more clinical than Sable, dissecting and rearranging information like a capable computer, then spitting out the options. "Hmm, might not be a bad idea at that," she mused. "That way he can't renege on the deal."

Sable's breath came out in a relieved whoosh. "That's right."

"Say," Talia began again, still frowning. "You're not thinking of shipping me off to boarding school, are you? It's bad enough that I have to move before my senior year. I want my family with me wherever I am."

Sable relaxed and let herself smile. "No one is putting you anywhere. You'll be with me, just like we always planned," she stated firmly.

Talia relaxed but persisted with her concerns. "It's just that I could understand if you wanted a year or so to get accustomed to this, uh, new arrangement."

"There's nothing to get used to, darling. This is a marriage of convenience. Nothing more." Sable's voice was calm. At least she knew what she was talking about on this subject.

"Okay." Her little sister shrugged, but Sable knew she was relieved. "So what happens next?"

"Next the movers begin packing our belongings tomorrow morning. On Friday we leave for Texas. All of us."

"Have you told your esteemed in-laws yet?"

"Not yet. Not until Friday morning."

Talia grinned. "Don't shoot the in-laws till you see the whites of their eyes."

"Remember the Alamo," Sable retorted, wondering if it was going to be her dying cry.

With Joe Lombardi on her side, could anyone be sure who would win the war?

SUNDAY WAS BEAUTIFUL, perfect for a wedding. The sun was buttery bright, but not too hot, and a light breeze soothed like gentle fingers.

Sable stared at herself in the mirror and wondered why she was so nervous. Looking calm and collected, the woman in the mirror stared back. At least her usual façade was still in place, even though her stomach churned.

Her wedding dress was of pale aqua silk, her hat a gauzy material that matched the dress and shoes. Simplicity and style, perfect for her height and figure.

Sensing the doubts running through Sable's mind, Talia gave her sister a hug. "You're a knockout," she stated with just a touch of envy.

"Thanks." Sable forced a smile. "I needed that."

"I don't know why. You're gorgeous. And the groom is a perfect match. He's so handsome."

Sable faced her sister. "You've seen him?"

"Yes. He's tall, dark and exciting. What he does to a tuxedo could only be described in a romance novel."

Romance novels were Sable's weakness. She read them by the ton and Talia knew it.

"That good, huh?"

"That good. He's dy-na-mite. And just as nervous as you are."

"I'm not—" Sable began, then stopped, unable to deny the emotion that was turning her bones into putty. "Is everyone here?"

"It looks like it. The place is crawling with people."

"Do you recognize anyone?"

"Well, it looks like everyone from the guest list is here, including your attorney and his secretary, along with two women from the foundation office," Talia reported. "The rest are all Joe's friends and business associates. Plus a few characters." Talia chuckled. "There's a bald-headed, bowlegged man who's got the face of Gabby Hayes and the voice of the Strangler. Joe calls him Totty, which should be the name of a chic model—or a Barbie doll's best friend."

Sable nodded, smiling at her sister's astute comment. She hadn't invited anyone other than those Talia had mentioned. "Are the caterers having any more problems? They couldn't decide where to set up the tents earlier."

Talia shook her head. "No. They set up the tents in the front. And the makeshift kitchen is a marvel to behold."

"No one's bothered me for the past hour," Sable said, suddenly worried. "Are you sure everything's okay?"

"Promise." Talia crossed her heart.

A knock on the door stopped Sable from asking more questions.

"Mrs. LaCroix? The minister says it's time." One of the maids hired for the occasion stood just outside the doorway with a warm smile of admiration. "And you do make a beautiful bride."

Sable smiled gratefully. "Thank you. I'll be right there." As the woman backed out, Sable stopped her. "Wait," she said. "Your sister is taking care of Johnny, isn't she?"

The woman nodded. "He's taking his nap right now, but when he wakes, she'll feed and play with him for a while, then bring him down to the reception."

"Tell her thank you again for me, will you?"

"I will," the maid promised. "And don't worry. She's raised three of her own. She knows what to do."

When the door closed, Sable took another deep breath and smiled. "Are you ready, Sis?"

"Ready," Talia answered, brushing the skirt of her pale peach dress. She looked much older than her seventeen years, Sable reflected. But luckily Talia still thought that meeting boys was a game. She hadn't yet reached the stage of regarding them as trophies to be won. Sable hoped things stayed that way for a little while longer. Talia had grown up so fast in so many other ways, it was nice to know that boys weren't part of the picture—yet.

"Let's go!" Sable declared with bravado. All the way down the hall to the living room, she prayed she was doing the right thing. Doubts assailed her from all directions, and they all centered on her husband-to-be.

Her gaze locked with Joe's. He stood by the side of the fireplace, his expression as stern as a schoolteacher's. Then suddenly he winked. With an inward sigh of relief she smiled, calm once more as she placed her hand in his. They turned toward the minister to speak their vows.

ALL OF JOE'S DOUBTS about the marriage hit him with stunning force, when he turned and saw Sable standing in the living room doorway.

She was beautiful. More than beautiful. Every man's dream of a bride. And she was his. Not to touch. Not to share. Just to give her his name. He had even signed a contract to that effect earlier that morning.

How was she going to manage, now that she was out of her own, exclusive element? This was no cosmopolitan city, not even a suburb. It was just a ranch house in a rural area. And she looked as if she couldn't swat a fly, let alone run a household or keep the home fires burning for her tired and overworked man to return to.

The second thought that came to mind astounded him.

She was an orchid. He was just a plain old wildflower. The two didn't go into the same corsage, let alone grow side by side.

This is a business marriage. Remember? he chided himself. But it didn't work. When she walked across the room and gave him her hand, his clasp was as light as a cobweb; he was afraid of hurting her.

Women like her belonged in the big city. Every woman he ever dated had sooner or later tried to get him to move to where the action was, in downtown Houston. Sable wouldn't be any different.

Afterward, others told him the marriage vows were perfect. But he didn't hear a word, didn't see anyone except Sable. He didn't give a damn about anything but getting through the ceremony. He was waiting for the kiss.

Then it was time and he got to do what he wanted. Joe lifted her veil and stared into eyes that were as uncertain as his. As vulnerable as a child's. As sensuous as those of a fully grown woman.

He was trapped. He knew it. And right now he didn't care.

His lips captured and held hers. He'd promised himself that it would be a short kiss, a kiss to seal their bargain. But he betrayed himself.

When his lips touched hers, every muscle in his body tightened to the breaking point. He forgot there was an audience, a minister, as his fingers tightened on her tiny waist. He pulled her closer, fitting her slender frame to his own hard body.

Her resisting hands scorched his chest as she pushed, to no avail. It took several seconds before he realized she was trying to push him away. He raised his head and stared down at her, his breath coming in short puffs.

Her eyes were enormous. "Joe," she whispered. "Everyone's waiting."

Her voice sounded like he felt: high and strung tight. But her words finally penetrated the fog in his brain. With a glance around the room, he pulled away.

Clearing his throat, he turned to the gathering. "Friends, may I introduce my wife, Sable LaCroix Lombardi."

The crowd clapped.

Still holding her hand tightly in his, Joe thanked the minister. Mike was best man and Talia had acted as bridesmaid. Suddenly Joe was glad his buddy was close by. He needed to get away from Sable if he was to think clearly.

Actually he needed a drink.

The guests engulfed them, expressing congratulations and good wishes, laughing, kissing and shaking hands. It was a nice feeling, one made nicer by the fact that those same people were separating him from Sable. Distance was imperative if he was at least to get his body under control. His mind might never be the same.

As his heartbeat evened out and his body relaxed, Joe returned to his senses. The desire to possess his new wife was still at the forefront, but he could handle it. It was just the nature of the situation, he told himself. Any man was allowed to become aroused on his wedding day—even if his wife was a nag. And Sable was not a nag. She was a thoroughbred.

Smiling as he made his way through the crowd of guests, Joe headed for the bar and ordered a beer. Sipping it, he watched the people surrounding his bride. Obviously she was bred to gracious hostessing. Their faces told him she'd charmed them, just as she had charmed him.

Wishing he was in his favorite jeans and shirt, he ran a finger around the collar of his tuxedo shirt. He wished he was in the barn. He'd never felt more like mucking out a stall so much in his life as he did right now.

Propping an elbow against the portable bar, he wrapped his fingers around the cold mug and frowned across the room at his new wife.

Mike came and stood beside him. "Congratulations, Joe. Sable is quite some woman."

"To say nothing of her million," Joe stated dryly, attempting to maintain his role as cynic.

"You mean to tell me you married her only because of her money?" Mike's voice was filled with disbelief.

"Of course," Joe declared evenly. "You ought to know. You arranged this little merger."

Mike grinned. "You might want to believe that tripe, but I know better. You couldn't have been hog-tied into marriage unless you wanted to be hog-tied. And that kiss was hardly platonic. The room temperature went up ten degrees."

Angry with himself for having revealed so much, Joe managed a shrug. "So what? She's a beautiful woman. I'm a normal man. End of story."

"Beginning of romance," Mike murmured, focusing his eyes on the group in the middle of the room.

Joe followed his friend's gaze. His eyes locked with bewitching, brown ones. Sable's expression was enigmatic, but somehow he knew that she was just as scared as he was.

The room full of guests disappeared. Only he and Sable remained. Joe couldn't turn away, couldn't look away. He couldn't do anything except remain caught in her gaze.

You kissed me as if you meant it, her eyes seemed to say.

You're beautiful. It's our wedding day, he answered.

But this is a business deal, not a springtime romance!

Did you like it? he questioned.

Too much.

So did I.

We shouldn't.

Let's pretend that we are really man and wife. Just for today. Let's be as happy for us as our friends are.

And when our friends leave?

The day is over.

And so is the game of Let's Pretend?

Yes.

Her sadness was as palpable as his own. Joe tried to convince himself that her responses were only in his imagination, but when he held out his hand to her in silent invitation, Sable responded by walking to his side and placing her hand in his. Her smile would have melted the hardest of hearts, but it was given to him.

People came up to them, and once more they played host and hostess. This time they stood together, holding hands. Both seemed content with the arrangement.

TALIA STUDIED Joe's young attorney and good friend. She had stood with him in front of the minister, unnoticed, acting as maid of honor to his best man. It didn't matter that he wasn't aware of her. He would be. She'd see to that. After all, she always got what she wanted. And she wanted Mike.

HER HAND firmly encased in Joe's, Sable smiled and chatted with their guests. But her mind was working overtime, replaying the earlier episode between Joe and herself.

When she'd looked up and met his admiring gaze, she'd been relieved. *Am I doing all right?* she had asked him silently.

You're doing fine, his look had answered. *I'm proud of the way you're handling everything.*

Then help me, she had requested. *Make certain that those who will carry details of the wedding back to Jonathan's grandparents in Louisiana will be satisfied with our motives.*

He'd held out his hand—and she'd been both relieved and sad. He was willing to help—but the whole day was a farce. They weren't in love. They weren't looking forward to spending the rest of their lives together. They were acting out parts in a play.

But right now that didn't matter. For the first time since she'd overheard the attorney and her now ex-in-laws discussing Jonathan's custody, the panic had subsided.

Everything was going to be all right. She knew it.

TALIA MADE HER WAY over to Mike, who was watching the guests as if he were conducting the orchestra, rather than being an item on the program.

"Nice crowd. Do you know everyone?" she asked.

Startled out of his reverie, Mike looked down at her. "Talia, isn't it?"

An impish smile played around her mouth. She nodded. "Since I was born."

"Which couldn't have been all that long ago."

His words were meant to emphasize the age difference between them. "Lucky, aren't I?" she queried lightly. "I still have the best years of my life ahead of me."

Again he looked startled. "Right," Mike finally drawled. "I wouldn't want to go through all those years again if I had a choice. It was too riddled with doubts and problems, to say nothing of acne."

Her smile grew broader. So he *was* interested. But her age was a definite drawback. "I agree on the problems and doubts. But I'll learn the answers with time. As for acne, I have no idea. I've never had it."

Mike laughed. "Does your sister know how precocious you are?"

"Alas, yes. She also knows my habit of going after what I want. Hence the nickname Spike, after a pit bulldog we knew."

He clearly understood her message. Mike took a step back. "I hope you're old enough to have learned to pursue only sure things."

"That's right." Her eyes twinkled with delight. "And the older I get, the more discerning I'll become."

He nodded sagely, but his eyes still held that wary look. "That's right."

"However," Talia added and grinned mischievously. "Wisdom doesn't automatically come with age."

"Then I'd ask someone older for advice. Your sister would have sound thoughts on the matter."

"What matter?" she asked innocently.

"Any matter," he snapped, obviously unnerved by what she was intimating, yet not sure if he was reading her correctly.

"Oh." She breathed slowly, then smiled at him again. "Well, it's been nice talking to you, Mike. I know we'll see each other often."

She turned to leave, but his hand lightly captured her arm. "Often?" he repeated.

"Yes. Didn't you know? I'm living here, too."

She was aware of his gaze on her as she walked away. Mike was twenty-eight, young for a man in his position. Her age was the problem. But eleven years weren't an insurmountable problem. Time and persistence would overcome his reservations. Sooner or later Mike would be hers.

ALL THE GUESTS, catering people and maids had left. Jonathan was sleeping, and Talia had gone off to her bedroom. The house seemed curiously empty.

Joe felt as empty as the house. Mike, thinking he already knew, had told Joe about his permanent "houseguest." Sable hadn't said a word—that was what hurt.

He didn't mind Talia living with them. It was the fact that Sable had purposely failed to mention it. He should have been consulted, dammit!

Sable was in the kitchen. It was time for a confrontation.

"Sable?" he called, pushing open the swinging door.

"Don't shout," she said calmly, putting a glass into the now pristine cupboard before turning to face him. "Johnny's asleep."

Her last words stabbed him deeply. He'd been married six hours, and already they sounded like an old, married couple. Her child was now his responsibility, too.

"Why didn't you tell me Talia was part of the package deal?" Instead of anger, he heard the soft query in his own voice.

Her gaze dropped to the floor. "I'm sorry. I should have, but I was afraid you might call off our... agreement."

"So I had to find out from Mike that you two are a pair?"

She nodded, her expression so contrite that he couldn't find the fury he had initially felt. "I was going to tell you now, only Mike beat me to it."

He leaned a hip against the wall, reminding himself not to go near her, or he might repeat the wedding kiss. That would never do. "What's the deal?"

"Talia is my sister," she said simply.

"And?"

"I've raised her this far, and I intend to continue to do so. John understood this, so I assumed you would, too."

Joe stood up straight. "First of all," he stated, "don't assume. I'm not John. You married him under different circumstances. I don't give a flying bat's wing what John understood. I'm the partner in this deal, not him. You should have been up-front with me." He ran a hand through his hair, his anger returning, though now it was tempered with caution.

"Look," he began again. "I understand your desire to have your sister with you. I just wanted to be told before the rest of the world knew. If John had been here to tell me about this, I wouldn't be in this situation— you'd still be married to him."

She looked as if he'd struck her, but he couldn't take back his words. They had to establish their relationship, and it had to be done now. "From now on, tell me what's going on before it happens," he told her, then waited in a cold sweat for her answer.

"You're right, of course," she finally agreed. "No one should go into a business deal without knowing all the facts. I'm sorry."

He raised his brows. "Is there anything else you've forgotten to tell me?"

"Such as?"

"Visitors? Other relatives who might want to move in?"

"No. None," she said softly, looking as guilty as a child caught playing hooky.

He wanted to comfort her. He wanted to kiss her. He wanted to bury himself in her and claim her as his own. Instead he nodded perfunctorily. "Good night."

"Good night."

He barely heard her answer; he practically ran down the hall. Closing the door behind him, he plopped onto the bed and cradled his head in his hands.

This was his wedding night. Something he'd always looked forward to. Yet here he was, sitting on his bed alone and wondering what the hell the rest of this marriage was going to bring. He couldn't act like a normal bridegroom and celebrate his own wedding. Instead, he was alone and insanely jealous of a man who, when he was alive, had been his best friend.

It was a hell of a way to spend a wedding night.

SABLE LET OUT HER BREATH in relief. She'd done it. She'd told him about Talia. Well, it had come out. So he'd found out before she could tell him. The result was the same. And though he had blustered, he'd also agreed.

She thought back over the wedding. The few guests she'd invited would go back to Louisiana and let her now ex-in-laws know the details. They'd been impressed with Joe, she could tell. When young Jonathan had come down to the party, Joe had made him laugh by talking nonsense. At that moment she'd known her decision to buy Joe as a bridegroom and a father for her child had been the right one.

She seriously doubted that the LaCroix family would try for custody now. But just in case, her attorney in Louisiana was keeping his ears open, ready to block any efforts they made. Now that she was living in Texas, instead of Louisiana, the LaCroix would have to file their suit here, and their influence didn't reach this far.

Her attorney had also informed her that Texas had a grandparents' law, one which stated that grandparents had the right to see their grandchildren, whether parents approved or not. And most states honored that law. That was all right with her. She had always given John's parents the right to see him, just not the right to raise him.

With a smile and a light heart, Sable flicked off the kitchen light and made her way to her bedroom. After checking on her son, she climbed into bed and sank into the plush pillows.

Remembering this was her wedding night, she had a momentary pang. Strange to be alone at such a time. Then, reminding herself that she'd found an excellent solution to her deepest fears, she smiled again.

Her smile still in place, she picked up one of the newest romances she'd bought and opened it. She settled deeper into the pillows and began to read.

Things couldn't have been better.

4

SUNLIGHT POURED through Sable's bedroom window. Pale peach percale sheets tangled around her legs as she rolled onto her back. With a groan of protest she pulled a pillow over her head to dull the light. But she didn't succeed in suppressing the sounds of Jonathan and Talia's laughter; both were apparently having a whale of a time in a pillow fight.

Children had absolutely no respect for an adult's exhaustion. This was the day after her wedding. One of the most tense days she'd ever lived through. Didn't they realize that? Apparently not, her fuzzy mind answered.

Opening one eye, she glanced at her watch, then bolted straight up in bed. It was after eleven in the morning! Within five minutes she was dressed in slacks and shirt and out of the bedroom, moving toward the sound of the ongoing pillow fight. Surprisingly, she felt terrific.

"Well, good morning, you two." She grinned.

Both were children; there was just a difference in size and sex. Talia's hair was sticking out all over her head, while Jonathan's pajamas, unsnapped at the back waist, drooped over his little bottom.

Jonathan stopped in midjump, his bright eyes wide and round as he tried to judge his mother's mood. Sable's grin grew larger, telling him he wasn't in trouble—this time. He giggled, then stuck his thumb into his mouth.

Talia ran one hand through her hair, attempting to tame her wild curls. "Hi. I thought you were sleeping."

"I was, until I heard the fun you two were having."

Talia glanced guiltily at the little tyke. "Were we loud? Did we wake up Joe, too?"

"I don't know," Sable said slowly, unwilling to admit that she had forgotten about him in her rush to see her family. "I'll go check. Meanwhile, how about you two getting dressed? I'll make breakfast."

"Brunch," Talia called after her.

"Pancakes!" Jonathan shouted.

"Prune juice," Talia substituted, knowing that was his least favorite drink.

Jonathan protested.

Although she halted before Joe's closed door, Sable wasn't brave enough to open it and see if he was still sleeping. She continued into the kitchen, hoping he'd be in there.

She was greeted by a note, in strong, masculine handwriting, propped up on the table. As Sable read, her hand tightened on the paper, practically crushing it.

I leave for the track around seven every morning. I like coffee and toast for breakfast. I'm usually home around noon, except for today. I've got a lunch appointment.

I'll be back around six or six-thirty for a hot meal. I'm a meat and potatoes man and I like to eat early so I can do my paperwork at night. Tonight we'll discuss your budget for the house and the type of meals I want. I let you sleep this morning, but I do expect you to be up when I am.

Sable read it again. Anger seared her body. The man had a way with words. Then she balled the message in her hand and threw it against the wall, watching it land on top of the refrigerator.

"We'll discuss my budget all right, my dear husband. But not on your timetable!" She gritted her teeth as she uttered the words. "And not until you learn some manners—how to request with sugar instead of vinegar, for example!"

The rest of the day was spent organizing rooms and belongings. The movers had brought in everything she needed, but not everything she wanted. Boxes still stacked in the garage had to be emptied.

She made at least four lists of things she needed to find or buy. At three o'clock Sable piled Talia and Johnny into the station wagon and headed toward Huntsville, where she had been assured was a large grocery store.

With a little forethought, she bet she could find enough shopping to keep her busy until way after "six or six thirty." By that time Joe would have returned home to find *her* note propped on the kitchen table beside a foil-wrapped roast beef sandwich, a can of cream of potato soup and a can opener.

He wanted meat and potatoes? He'd get meat and potatoes! At least two weeks' worth!

JOE PACED THE KITCHEN with Sable's note clenched in his fist. The food he'd found beside her message was untouched.

The message was short and to the point.

I've taken Talia and Jonathan grocery shopping in Huntsville. Like a dutiful wife I'll cook your meals, but it must be done with the proper ingredients. There are none in this kitchen.

I can't wait to return so we can have our "discussion."

P.S. Salt and pepper are not the only ingredients with which to cook.

She was angry. It hadn't been hard to find his balled-up note to her on the top of the fridge. It stood out in the spotless kitchen.

All right, so he'd been reprimanded. It wasn't until he'd read his note through her eyes that he realized how abrupt it was. But what did she expect?

The telephone had woken him before dawn with Totty on the other end, telling him that Ahab had won the race. Not realizing the businesslike relationship Joe and Sable had, Totty had assumed Joe could not be disturbed last night—his wedding night.

He'd been in a hurry when he'd written that note.

Besides, he dealt with men all day long, and the best and easiest way with them was to be as direct as possible. That way no one misunderstood. Admittedly he needed a little practice in dealing with women. He could keep up good manners as well as the next man, but this woman was now his wife. Did he have to have good manners forever?

He knew the answer. At least he could try. His foster mother used to say that good manners were the same as courtesy, and courtesy was the same as respect. He certainly respected Sable and the capable way she handled both the toddler and a headstrong, teenage girl. And he'd tell her so as soon as he could.

So why wasn't she home yet? His six-or-six-thirty deadline had passed more than three hours ago. Now he was concerned. He refused to think of the word "scared."

But he couldn't stop picturing the possibilities. Her car could have broken down. She could have had an accident. He didn't know if she carried their phone number with her. Did she even have the address? If something had happened to them, who would know to contact him? All her identification probably still carried the Louisiana address.

Unable to wait any longer, he reached for the kitchen phone to call the police. Just then, car headlights angled down the driveway. Relief flooded through him as he recognized Sable's car.

By the time she entered the house, he had worked himself up again for a major confrontation. The only thing that made him hold his tongue was Johnny was asleep in Sable's arms. Talia was right behind her sister, carrying their purses and a large bag of groceries.

Sable met his gaze. Signaling to him to be quiet, she continued down the hall to the child's room. Joe had no recourse but to follow Talia to the kitchen.

"What happened?" he demanded. "Did the car break down?"

"We got lost," Talia answered, wearily dropping the grocery bag onto the kitchen table. "It seemed like we were wandering around forever."

He'd thought of everything but that. "How long were you lost?" He softened his tone. Talia looked as if she was about to cry. She didn't need to hear his own frustrated anger.

"Since about six. Somehow we got the farm-to-market roads mixed up and we took the wrong one. When we realized it, it was dark and we stopped for directions. Nobody seemed to know exactly where we wanted to go, but they all had ideas."

"The roads aren't hard to follow. You'll get used to them soon."

"It's not Louisiana," Talia told him, sniffing. "We were all tired, and none of these darn roads are marked, except for an occasional sign you have to get out of the car to read, 'cause it's so dark. I never would have gotten lost at home."

Joe had a feeling most of Talia's reaction was due to moving to a new place. And it had put a strain upon everyone, something he'd not considered while worrying about how his life was being changed by the marriage. Three other people had gone through changes, too.

Joe watched Talia, tears of frustration sheening in her eyes as she began to automatically empty the bag of groceries. Overwhelmed by a feeling of protectiveness, he reached out and gave her a sympathetic pat on the back. Her slight shoulders quaked as she accepted his comfort. A moment later she looked up, giving him a brilliant smile that reminded him of her older sister.

"Thanks," she said, rising on tiptoe to place a kiss upon his cheek.

"You're welcome." He felt awkward somehow, not quite sure how to respond. "Are there more groceries in the car?"

"Plenty," she confirmed, putting cans into the cupboard. "I don't understand it. For a woman who only eats fish and chicken, we've got more meat and potatoes than you can shake a stick at."

Joe grinned. Sable might have been angry, but at least she paid attention to his requests. "I'll get them."

After he carried in the last of the bags, Joe felt Sable's presence as surely as if she'd tapped him on the shoulder.

He turned. Her tired eyes were half-closed, her lips slightly parted. Her shoulders drooped with the sheer effort of standing.

"Hi," he said softly. He wanted to hold her. He wanted to give her the comfort of his body as much as he needed the comfort of hers. But he wasn't sure how to go about it.

"Hi," she repeated.

"You okay?"

"We got lost."

Joe nodded. "Talia told me all about it. It was the one thing I didn't think of."

Her glance was rueful. "Frankly, neither did I, but everything looked different as the sun set. Then all those tall pines made the narrow road look even narrower."

"How did you finally manage to get here?"

"I went back to town and retraced my steps, trying not to look at anything but the lefts and rights."

Relieved, Joe let out a pent-up breath. At least they were safe. "I'll get you an up-to-date map of the area. That should help. I'll also make sure you have all the phone numbers you need. You could have called me earlier on the car phone or pager."

She closed her eyes for a moment. "I didn't have any numbers on me, including the house phone. I didn't even have the address. It's in my briefcase. It didn't dawn on me that you had a car phone."

"I figured that," he said gently.

She opened her eyes and stared up at him. "Were you worried? Or were you angry?"

He grinned sheepishly. "Both. But I was worried most."

"I'm sorry. I didn't mean for this to happen."

"It won't again. I should have given you all the information before you needed it." He stood in front of her. "I'll write it all down in the morning and put it into both glove compartments. That way neither you nor Talia will get lost again."

"Thank you," she said, stifling a yawn.

He smiled. "Why don't you go on to bed? Talia and I can put away the rest of the stuff."

"It's already done," Talia announced with a tired grin. She folded the last bag and placed it with the others in the utility room.

"Thanks," Sable said. "I'm on my way."

For a brief moment her eyes locked with Joe's. Both stood completely still.

Then Joe moved to break the spell. "Good night," he said gruffly.

"Good night," Sable answered, turning to go back to her room.

"Oh, and Sable?" Joe called. She glanced over her shoulder at him. "When I said meat, I didn't mean just beef. Chicken and fish are fine, too. Occasionally."

She smiled and his blood warmed, flooding his body with feelings best left alone.

"I'll remember that," she murmured, then disappeared down the hallway and into her room.

Joe whistled softly as he pulled a beer from the fridge. He'd been too crass and too abrupt with Sable. He needed to try a little tenderness, as the old song said. He'd get more from her if he treated her with a little respect.

How much more? the devil in his mind asked. A real marriage? His make-believe wife in his very real bed? He pushed that thought aside. He'd signed the contract for money, and that had been what he got: enough to finish his beloved racetrack.

"Good night," Talia called.

Joe jumped guiltily, as if the thoughts plaguing him were written across his forehead for everyone to see.

"Good night," was the best he could manage. Those other, more provoking thoughts would have to wait. Right now he was starved, and there was no one around to cook for him. He unwrapped the sandwich Sable had fixed for him earlier and took a healthy bite.

Not bad. Not bad at all.

BY THE NEXT MORNING the truce was over.

"I support my family, Sable. Not you. And we'll live within my means." His tone brooked no argument. "It's worked for hundreds of generations, and it's gonna work in this marriage, too."

Sable's back straightened. Her tension was palpable. "Joe," she began, slowly turning to face him. "If I were working at a job in town, would I be allowed to participate in paying the bills? In buying things for the house?"

His look was wary. "Yes, but you're not working—not that way." He held up a hand to forestall her triumph. "And you're married to me. That means that I take care of you."

"No," she declared, equally firm in her beliefs. "It means I'm married to you. No more, no less. I can still spend my money any way I see fit. That was the purpose of our prenuptial agreement—our separate property remains our separate property. You have no right to tell me how to spend my money or when I can spend it."

"This is my house and you're my wife. You will live within my means," Joe maintained. "I pay bills and groceries. The rest you can handle."

"There is no 'rest' after those two things!"

"Exactly."

His look was so smug that Sable could barely control her intense desire to kick him.

"And while we're on the subject of duties, I think we'd better get some things straightened out between us," Joe went on, obviously determined to bull his way through this meeting.

"Such as what?" Now it was her turn to be wary.

"Such as who takes care of your three horses."

She raised her brows. "And who does?"

"You do. My crew has enough to do without adding to their work load. You can groom them and muck out their stalls. After all, you're home all day."

"I hate horses. I kept them only because I thought the fillies might breed a winner. The colt is Jonathan's when he gets older."

"You take care of them, except for the feed and exercise. The men can do that when they're handling the other horses."

"Anything else?" she queried sarcastically.

"That's it." Joe folded his arms over his broad chest and smiled.

She knew he was waiting for fireworks to go off, but she wouldn't give him the satisfaction of seeing her lose her temper.

Instead she smiled sweetly. "Then I have a few dos and don'ts for you. First, you gave me the schedule for meals, so I expect you to abide by it. All meals will be on time, and unless you call and let me know you won't be home, you'll be sitting at the table when I serve them."

Joe frowned, but nodded in agreement.

"Next, let me remind you that this is our home, not the bunkhouse. No more boots on the furniture or sweaty hats on the chairs. That goes for all your employees, too."

"What makes you think we do that?"

"Because no coffee table could be so scuffed, unless a thousand pairs of boots had rested there."

Again he nodded agreement, and the light blush on his cheeks confirmed her assessment of the situation.

"And lastly, no heavy drinking."

Joe opened his mouth to protest, but shut it again. "Fair enough. But I can't and won't control what goes on in the bunkhouse. None of the men are drunks, but they can drink what they want to, when they want to, as long as it's not on the job. I'm their boss, not their father."

"Fair enough," she mimicked.

Joe unfolded his arms and glanced at his watch. "Now that we've gotten that out of the way, I've got to get to work. Is there anything else you need clarified?"

He deserved a slap. He deserved a punch! He was always so cocksure and arrogant!

She clamped her hands on her hips to stop herself turning thoughts into deeds. "And what are my other duties, master?" she inquired in a taunting tone.

"The usual things any normal wife does." He stopped, letting his gaze feed on her mouth. "With the exception of the one thing that seems so repugnant to you, of course," he finally said. "According to our contract, you're not required to be in my bed."

His derisive tone hurt. The fact was that she was beginning to wish she hadn't stipulated that they weren't to sleep together. Her pride had been the main reason. Did she have to pay him to sleep with her, too?

"If I recall, you didn't seem to mind that addendum at the time."

"You were offering me a million dollars, darlin'," he drawled, clearly intent on giving as good as he got. "Was I supposed to disagree with the basic terms?"

"You could have."

This time it was his turn to move away. "It seemed like a good idea back then. It just isn't reality now. It's unnatural for two people, married or not, to live in the same house and not consummate the relationship."

"What's unnatural about it?" Sable found herself asking. "I have my room, you have yours. That way there is no temptation."

Joe shrugged as if dismissing the thought. "Fine. I'm not arguing the point. We both agreed. I'm just saying that it's hard to act as if this is a marriage made in heaven, when it hasn't been *made* at all."

The bluntness of his accusation slapped her in the face. The worst part was that she knew he was right. How could either of them act naturally as a couple, when a major portion of the marriage—the bed—was not being shared?

She didn't have an answer. With determined steps she walked to the door. "You pay the bills and groceries. I cover the rest," she repeated, as if nothing else had been said. "Now I've got laundry to do. Excuse me."

"You're excused," he muttered before she was out the door. "And dammit, you're stubborn, to boot."

SABLE KEPT HERSELF BUSY in the laundry room until she heard Joe's truck driving off. She'd been afraid of what else she might say or do if she remained in the same room with him.

Didn't he know how degrading it was to have to buy oneself a husband? The few men she'd known in Louisiana had run in her in-laws' circle. And they had treated her as if she were not to be touched.

At first she hadn't minded. Her memories of John and the constant attention the baby and Talia had needed made up a full and busy life. Contrary to what society thought of her, she'd always been happiest at home. She loved the quiet atmosphere, the little things that constantly needed to be done for the smooth running of a house. It had been John who insisted she attend public events and join charities. She had continued with those obligations to fill the lonely void John's death had created.

But at night she roamed her house with no one to talk to. Her in-laws were not people she could turn to to assuage her solitude. She had had no one to laugh with, to talk over problems with. She had no man to love.

She wanted to repeat the best moments of her marriage with John—when she'd curled next to him in bed and talked about the things that bothered her, and he'd soothed her with his gentle, caring touch.

She missed that the most.

Joe was another matter entirely. Joe didn't comfort her, he excited her. She wanted to touch him, feel his skin next to hers. She wanted to make love to him. And that was scary. She'd never felt that way before, and she didn't want to now.

With Joe everything was physical. His look, his words, even his voice seemed to touch the very core of her. He made her think of things best left alone.

Alone in bed at night, her imagination ran riot, exploring what she refused to think about during the day. Like the way his hands might feel on her body. Like curling next to him in bed and talking about the day's happenings, while he stroked her back and waist and placed small, butterfly kisses upon her forehead and cheek. Like his possession of her, and her triumph over his carefully controlled emotions. . . .

She'd obviously been reading too many romances.

She took a deep breath and straightened her spine. This wasn't getting her anywhere. With determined movements, she placed the rest of the clothes in the washer and set the dials.

Keep busy. That was the answer.

"Is Joe gone?" Talia asked as she and Jonathan came in from a walk around the property. The boy ran to her, and Sable picked him up, giving him a big hug and a kiss under his chin. He laughed in response, his chubby little hands pushing hard against her.

"Yes," Sable said as she put him down.

"And did you have a good discussion?"

"Yes."

"And who won?" Talia continued as she set the grubby Jonathan on the counter and began taking off his muddy sneakers. It was too late for the kitchen floor, but he could still make a mess of the recently cleaned carpet. "Joe?"

Sable couldn't think of an answer, so she continued to busy herself with the dirty clothes.

"Was it a dead heat?" Talia inquired, not allowing her sister any leeway.

"More or less."

Jonathan squirmed, nearly falling off the counter. Talia caught him, then let him stand in his stocking feet. Immediately he ran off down the hall toward his bedroom.

"I like him."

Sable went on trying to look busy, although for the life of her she didn't know what she was doing. "You'd better. He's probably the only nephew you'll ever have."

"No, I meant I like Joe."

Picking up a particularly dirty shirt, Sable placed it on top of the washer and treated it with a spot cleaner. Anything to stay busy. She was unwilling to look at Talia. "Do you?"

"Yes," Talia stated emphatically. Like all her decisions, she'd stick to it single-mindedly. "He's nice, he's funny and kind."

"You've gotten all that from three days of living in the same house with him?"

"That and more. Did you know that when I was almost on the verge of tears last night, he gave me a hug? Just like Dad—" Talia's voice broke off and she stared out the window.

She turned and faced Sable once more. "Why don't you go for broke, Sable, and make this a real marriage? One you could have kids in and enjoy? It beats all the fencing that's gone on in the past few days."

Sable looked her sister in the eye. There was no use in being subtle when it came to Talia. She refused to allow anyone to hide behind a facade. "It's none of your business, Talia, and there has been no fencing."

Talia eyed her sister. "Then why did I have to take Jonathan out of the house this morning, when he was shaken by you two shouting at each other?"

"He was upset?" Concern laced Sable's words. She'd had no intention of upsetting Jonathan. Nothing was worth that. After all, she ought to know. She'd experienced enough of it in her younger days.

"Yes, and it was your voice that was rising in anger. Not Joe's."

"You're living up to your nickname again, Spike," Sable warned.

"Yes, and the one who calls me that is more stubborn than me," Talia retorted.

"Only because the man's pigheaded." Sable stalked out of the utility room and into the kitchen, pouring herself a glass of water to soothe her dry throat.

"And so are you. But that doesn't mean the marriage couldn't be a real one. Jonathan could have sisters and brothers to enjoy." Talia's voice softened. "Johnny needs a family. Just like we did, Sable. Where would I have been without you?"

"He's got a family. You and me." In spite of Talia's look, Sable continued. "I'd do anything for you two," Sable said, her throat still dry and scratchy. "But I already bought myself a husband, Talia. I'm not about to purchase a baby as well. At that rate I'd be broke in no time. Jonathan will just have to live with being an only child."

"I know it was awful when Mom and Dad went to court over us, but that won't happen again, Sable—thanks to Joe. The LaCroix would have to be insane to file for custody. Don't you think this could work as a real family? For all of us?"

Sable swallowed. How could she explain that she simply couldn't grovel? What scraps of pride Sable had left, she wore like a full-length coat made of her namesake.

"I'll think about it."

Talia began to say something else, but the look on Sable's face stopped her. "I'll check on Jonathan," she said, hastily beating a retreat.

The large, black-and-white clock on the wall said it was only ten-thirty in the morning. Having already gone through two emotional scenes, she wished the day were over.

Her head tilted to one side, she continued to stare at the clock. It was definitely ugly, its black cord hung down the wall like a snake. Even if she had built her own prison, there was nothing in the agreement to say that she couldn't decorate it the way she wanted.

A sad smile crossed her lips. She knew the source of her frustration, but activity was the panacea. Activity was the one thing she could control.

5

EVEN BEFORE she opened the letter, she knew it contained bad news. The LaCroix insignia was on the flap of the envelope; it looked as intimidating as it was formal.

Johnny's grandparents wanted Sable to send the little boy to live with them, so they could place him in one of the best private preschools in Louisiana, ensuring that he would have the right friends and connections for his future. It wasn't so much a request as a demand.

Implied was a threat that if she didn't give up Johnny voluntarily, they would find a way to force her. Seething with fury, she was dialing their number to tell them exactly where they could put their fancy paper, when the truth dawned on her.

She had bought her security.

The LaCroix could threaten, but they couldn't win—not as long as she was married.

She would ignore the letter.

It would drive them crazy.

SABLE ENJOYED turning Joe's house into a home and having no one underfoot to tell her this was wrong or that would be better. It was the first time she'd ever had that luxury, and although the housework was constant, it was also a source of pride—and it kept her too busy to lure Joe to her bed.

She'd decided not to tell Joe about the letter. She was sure he wouldn't quite see it in the same light as she did. Jonathan was her child, and she knew what was best.

Joe seemed as wary of another confrontation as Sable was, so they stayed out of each other's way as much as possible. That allowed them to get along fine for the rest of the week and weekend.

But because he wasn't always around—because she missed him?—Sable noticed every little thing about him. At mealtimes, when they were forced to be together, she got to watch him up close. There were a thousand little items she hadn't known about the man, but enjoyed learning.

For instance, Sable was amazed by how firmly but gently Joe handled Jonathan. The boy quickly grew to worship his new father figure. He talked constantly as he followed Joe through the house, gardens and barns. And Joe never lost patience with him. In fact, Sable thought he enjoyed his new role.

Joe and Talia teased each other mercilessly. The rapport they had built was obvious to everyone. Talia went around the house singing Joe's praises until Sable had to tell her to stop or go to her room.

She couldn't have bought a better father figure if she'd tried.

But husband material . . . Joe was not.

He cussed like a cowboy. He never asked for her opinion. He never held her or whispered sweet nothings in her ear. He didn't seem to be interested in doing anything other than snarling at or ignoring her. He certainly wasn't like any of the heroes she'd read about in her romances—so why did she dream about him?

He scuffed the floor with his boots. His hats were always tossed carelessly onto a chair. He read the paper and invariably dropped it onto the floor. Rather than put his dirty clothes into the hamper in his bathroom, he left them on the floor behind the door, neatly piled, but on the floor nonetheless. And late at night he always raided the freezer for a bowl of ice cream—any flavor except chocolate. Then he'd leave the rinsed bowl in the sink, not the dishwasher.

It was disturbing—to her housekeeping and her psyche. She couldn't make a move without being reminded of Joe.

Every time she saw Joe's arms bared by a short-sleeved shirt, her heartbeat quickened. Images flashed through her mind of those same arms circling her waist, holding her close to his hard body. Even his long-legged stride reminded her of other, more intimate movements. She was beginning to wonder what pristine scruples were keeping her from Joe's bed.

But the bottom line was that she was afraid. No woman wanted to believe the only way a man would be interested in her was because she'd paid him for the services. And paid him dearly. No matter how many times she tried to forget that fact, it was there.

She'd bought a groom. She couldn't quite believe that he was as interested in her as he had been in her money.

She had to keep busy if thoughts of Joe's touch, Joe's kisses were to be overridden enough to allow her to function as a homemaker and mother.

Two kisses do not a fantasy make, she told herself—
and knew she lied.

JOE STOOD just inside the huge, barn doors and stared
at the house Sable had turned into a home. She had
done wonders, moving knickknacks here instead of
there, hanging a painting or print on a different wall,
and the room's whole complexion had been changed.
Even that big, ugly clock in the kitchen had been replaced by a brass-and-white thing that suited the area
much better.

As much as he hated to admit it, he was glad she'd
taken the house in hand. He liked it.

But swallowing those words wasn't his problem.
That would be easy compared to his one, big obstacle.

He wanted her. Day and night he wanted her. But
their stupid agreement was in the way.

From their first meeting Joe had been fascinated.
Then he'd been stunned. Sable had actually stated she'd
had no choice but to marry him! That had hurt his ego.
While they were getting to know each other better, he'd
honestly believed she was as drawn to him as he was to
her. The sparkle in her eyes when she looked at him
matched his own.

True, he had needed her money—money he vowed
he would pay back to her, if it was the last thing he did.
Only the pressure from the bank, his partners and Sable had forced him into this marriage.

That wasn't quite true.

No matter how much he lied to everyone else, he
couldn't lie to himself. Part of him, a large part, had

wanted this marriage. Otherwise wild horses couldn't have made him walk to the altar.

But that same damn money that was enabling him to finish building his track was also keeping him from his wife's bed. He saw dollar signs in her eyes every time he looked at her. He was sure she didn't think that way, but the fact that he'd been forced into taking the money was like a sore spot on his male pride. Whenever he thought of Sable, he also thought of the money he owed her.

His thoughts shifted to Jonathan and Talia, his ready-made family. Sable had thought she was pulling a fast one when she "forgot" to mention that her little sister was part of the deal. And he had to admit he hadn't been all that thrilled. But what he'd thought would be a hassle had turned out to be a joy. Talia was a bright, witty, older-than-her-age teenager. She didn't mind lending a hand with anything that needed doing, and her quick tongue was fun. And Jonathan...well, what could be wrong with an almost-three-year-old boy who had the good taste to idolize him?

The family was his. In such a short time they had learned to love him and he to love them. Now if he could only get Sable to follow their direction . . .

Joe groaned wearily and closed his eyes. All week long he had attended one business meeting after another until late into the night.

His maintenance chief had resigned because of a heart problem, and now he had to find a replacement. Interviews for the executive jobs had been squeezed between staff meetings, but he wasn't satisfied with the applicants. A friend had tipped him off that an out-of-state racetrack's chief wanted to return to Texas. Joe had called him, and the man had agreed to fly out for an interview today. They were to meet at the Houston Intercontinental Airport's private lounge tonight.

It was just one more pressure added to all the others. And all he could think about was a woman whose eyes matched her name. A woman who shared her money with him, but not her bed. He'd rather have had the bed.

There was only one thing to do. He had to forget about the money—until he could pay her back. Instead he would work on their relationship. When he gave her the money, he had to give her a reason to stay.

He had to seduce her. He had to woo her, as if she were a woman he'd just met and was...attracted to. He wouldn't allow himself to think of a stronger word. If he was to get any peace during the day and any sleep at night, he had to win her over to his way of thinking. Starting right away.

He could learn how to please her. But first he'd have to know what it was that made her smile, and the only way to do that was to spend time with her. If nature took its course while he was doing that, then all the better.

He found himself smiling. He stretched his arms high above his head in the cool shadows of the breezeway. He had a new challenge. He loved challenges.

SABLE SAT DOWN at the kitchen table and took a deep breath. She'd felt tired all week. Tired of fighting Joe. Tired of fighting with herself.

She'd been a waitress in one of Mobile's better restaurants when she'd met John. He'd sat at her table once, then returned again and again. She'd known he was wealthy. He'd known she wasn't.

After their marriage, a host of servants had taken care of their home. She'd been considered a socialite, but what she'd wanted most was to be a wife and mother, busy with the things wives and mothers did. Not a grand ambition, she'd be the first to admit, but it was hers. And somehow she'd always thought she'd do it for love of her family. Then she had discovered that being John's wife with nothing to do was boring.

Now she was twenty-six years old, and ironically this pretend marriage was the closest she'd ever come to fulfilling her dream.

She heard Joe's heavy-booted tread on the back porch steps, and her heart picked up its beat in anticipation. She remained seated, her ears following the sound of the motions she knew he was making. Then the door opened, he stepped in and smiled.

Her heart beat faster. She smiled back.

"Hi," she said, unable to remove the huskiness from her voice.

"You look bushed." His voice was low, sexy and sweetly concerned. He could read a feed list in that tone and she'd listen to every word.

"I'm a little tired," she admitted, suddenly not feeling quite as weary as she had before.

Joe glanced around at the sparkling counters, the spotless floor, the neat little decorations that made the kitchen glow with a country look. Then his gaze returned to her. "Where's Talia?"

She raised her brows questioningly. "She's reading in her bedroom."

"And Jonathan?"

"Taking a nap. He should be awake in a few minutes."

His smile expressed satisfaction. He pulled out the chair kitty-corner from her and sat down. Taking her hand, he interlaced his sun-darkened fingers with hers, his thumb rubbing sensuously against her palm.

"I have to go to the airport in Houston to interview a man."

"For employment at the track?"

"Yes. We lost our maintenance chief. This guy may take the job."

She nodded, suddenly wary. He usually announced his meetings in a most casual manner. This was anything but casual.

"Come with me."

Her eyes widened. "Now?"

It was his turn to nod.

"Why?"

"Because you've worked so hard since we got married, and I think you could use the break." His grin was endearing. "Besides, it's a long drive and I don't want to go alone. I'd rather have a quiet drink with you while I wait for the guy to arrive." He tightened his grip. "It'll do us both good to get away for a little while."

"But what about the kids?"

"Talia can baby-sit. If an emergency comes up, she only has to phone the bunkhouse and twelve men will come running."

"What about dinner?"

"We'll eat out. It won't hurt the kids to eat sandwiches for dinner this once."

"Give me half an hour."

"Fifteen minutes, or I'll come get you," he teased, his blue eyes crinkling at the corners.

Sable had a feeling that he'd do just that. "Twenty," she bargained.

"You're wasting your fourteen minutes." He stood and pulled her to her feet. Before she could react, he kissed the tip of her nose. "Twenty minutes," he whispered.

She felt buoyant. Her feet were at least six inches off the floor. "Twenty minutes," she promised before darting out the kitchen door and down the hall to her room.

Sable had never dressed so quickly. Knowing Joe was wearing exactly what he had on, she decided on peach-colored pants and a front-button summer sweater with nubby, silk leaves of copper, tan and green spilling over one shoulder. It was dressy, but not too much so. She put on low heels in the same shade of green. With deft fingers she twisted her dark hair and pinned it with a plain, gold barrette atop her head. Instead of her usual stud earrings, she chose gold hoops.

Exactly twenty minutes later she walked down the hall to Talia's room, only to find that Joe had already informed her sister of the impromptu arrangements.

"Have a great time," Talia called as she picked up a still-sleepy Jonathan and watched them climb into the jet-black truck and drive off.

Sable felt almost as if she'd been let out of jail, which wasn't really fair, she had to admit, since she'd chosen to remain at home this past week. She hated to acknowledge it, but she was happy because Joe had asked for . . . wanted . . . her company. It was a heady experience.

"You look wonderful." With a look of endearment, he touched the hand that rested on the seat between them. "Are you still tired?"

"I'm fine," she said with a laugh. "I'm just a little giddy at the thought of eating something I haven't cooked."

"You've been working too hard."

"No harder than you."

"It's different for me. The racetrack is my dream. My baby. Everything I have or ever wanted to have is tied up in it."

"The house and those who live in it make up my dream," she said softly. "Everything that matters to me is there."

"Touché," he murmured before releasing her hand and pulling onto the paved road that led to the interstate.

Sable leaned back and relaxed, watching the scenery pass by in a series of blurred, variegated greens. The ground was lush with last fall's leaves composting in the forest. And the ground gave off the scent of fresh earth and the tang of pine needles.

They passed through Conroe, the self-contained community of the Woodlands, and on down through Spring, another small town. Then they turned toward Houston's huge Intercontinental Airport.

Joe broke the companionable silence. "What are you thinking?"

"Just that I was amazed when I flew into the airport to visit you the first time and saw so many trees. I always thought Houston and the surrounding areas were in the middle of a prairie."

Joe chuckled. "Houston sits just south of the edge of Big Thicket, the largest, densest section of forest in the country. The Comanche Indians, runaway slaves and even a few well-known bandits used to hide there."

"I know," she said dryly. "It extends into Louisiana. I just didn't know it was down here, too."

Joe drove up the spiral ramp and parked in the garage attached to the airline terminal. With tender care he helped her from the car and toward the elevators that carried them to the lobby and the bar.

For the first time since the wedding, Sable felt like part of a married couple. Joe held her arm as he led her into the private, airline club room and toward a small table next to the wall. He ordered their drinks as if they'd been together for years.

Yes, she decided, they looked like an old married couple—until he looked at her.

His gaze was as hot as molten lava, burning her insides with its heat and stirring embers she thought long dead and forgotten. Her face flushed and her skin tingled.

His hand covered hers, cupping her fingers against the coolness of her wineglass. "You're beautiful," he told her softly. "You know that."

She swallowed the dryness that had attacked her throat. "It's nice to hear."

"You're the most beautiful woman I've ever seen."

"Thank you," she murmured, barely managing to speak. Her mouth was still as dry as a desert. Her mind told her she'd heard the words before, but they had never meant much to her. Now she wanted to hear more, craved more from him and yet felt guilty for the craving.

She couldn't stand seeing the desire in his blue eyes anymore and stared down at the glass in her hand—in their hands. His fingers interspersed with hers, made a pattern of light and dark against the gold-filled goblet. She could imagine their limbs entwining in the same golden aura and her heartbeat quickened. She was caught in a spell she couldn't shake.

Before she realized it, she had spoken the words. "You're weaving a spell around me."

The corners of his eyes crinkled. "I wish I could. At least as strong as the one you've woven around me."

Her eyes widened. "Have I?"

He nodded slowly. "Oh, yes. And I love it." His smile was like a breath of sunshine. "But I don't think the workers are too fond of me right now. I go around preoccupied. My mind is on you instead of my work."

She didn't know what to do so she pulled her hand away and entwined all ten fingers in her lap, so she couldn't be tempted to touch him.

"The racetrack will be ready soon." Her voice was unsteady, she knew, she was trying to focus her thoughts on anything but his nearness.

"Soon," he echoed in a husky voice.

"And then you can relax a little."

He nodded. "A little."

Her eyes darted to his, then back down to her glass. When he took his hand from the glass, she saw his fingerprints there. His clasp had made an impression against the chilled glass, just as it had on her entire being.

"Joe!" a man's voice called, and the spell was broken.

After the introductions, Joe began the interview. Sable leaned back and enjoyed the hum of conversation as the two men talked business. It was enlightening to listen to them and learn just a little more about the behind-the-scenes working of a racetrack. She had no idea there was so much to do or that so many people were involved. Joe's racetrack would give jobs to an area that had no industry of its own.

Sipping on her wine, she allowed her eyes to drift about the private bar and waiting room. It was tastefully finished with large, comfortable, padded chairs and small tables. Along the walls were desks, along with several copy machines and even a fax machine or two. Small, stylish telephones dotted the conversation tables. Everything about the room was expensive. Apparently only high-powered businessmen and -women could afford the dues to this private club. Sable was pleased to note that there seemed to be an almost equal number of men and women.

This was all new to her. She had never traveled much, and when she did it was in John's family plane, with no stopovers between their home in Louisiana and their destination.

Joe stood suddenly and shook hands with Mr. Tramore.

When the man held out his hand to Sable, she took it. "It was a pleasure meeting you, Mrs. Lombardi," he said.

"It was nice meeting you, Mr. Tramore," she said, startled by her own name. *Mrs. Lombardi.* It was the first time she'd really thought of herself as Joe's wife. It felt good.

The man tipped back his Western hat with two fingers. "Y'all be careful gettin' home," he growled as nicely as he could.

Sable couldn't hide her grin. Both he and Joe were apparently very similar when it came to women. Both were shy. But Joe hid his shyness by blustering, while this gentleman hid behind his manners.

"What's so funny?" Joe asked with a puzzled look as the man left the room.

"Men in general," she answered, still chuckling.

"And me in particular?" He took her arm and escorted her out of the room and into the large lobby.

When the elevator doors closed behind them and they were alone she whispered her answer. "Yes."

His eyes, focused on her, burned. She felt as if she'd just swallowed a rich, golden brandy. . . .

"Am I that funny?" His lips were mere inches from hers.

She shook her head slightly, moving her lips even closer to his. "No." The word came out as a breath that Joe stole.

"You're playing with me," he muttered. "Beware, Sable. Two can do that." His lips sealed hers, the pressure so slight that she leaned toward him for more. Her head reeled, but with strong hands anchored on her hips, he kept her firmly in place, letting her come no closer than he wanted her.

She wanted more. Ached for more. Craved for more.

Then the elevator doors opened. He pulled away and smiled benignly at the people grouped around the doors, waiting to get on.

As he escorted her off, he raised his voice so that it would carry to the others. "Lady, I'm sure you're every bit worth the two hundred you're asking, but I only have a ten on me."

"Forget it, then," she said just as loudly, walking away from him. "I'll just drive my Cadillac home. Good night, mister."

She felt Joe's hand on her shoulder and she turned to face him. "Don't ever do that to me again." Her voice was sweet and syrupy, but she knew her eyes blazed fire.

His jaw snapped shut. "No, ma'am. Never," he promised. "It was only a little joke."

"I won't be the butt of any man's joke. Not even yours."

"No, ma'am," he repeated as she stood in front of him. "I promise."

"Good. Now can we get something to eat? I'm starved!" She started toward their parked truck.

Joe followed without another word. It wasn't until they were in the cab of the truck that they looked at each other and Joe began to chuckle.

"Why did you go along with me?"

She shrugged, holding back a smile. "It seemed like the thing to do. I wasn't about to let you have the last word."

Then, seeing his expression, Sable couldn't help it. She chimed in. A few seconds later they were both laughing until tears streamed down their cheeks.

"Lady," he said when he caught his breath. "You're full of surprises. I would have thought you'd be at a loss for words. Instead you one-upped me."

"It's only fair," she told him between chuckles.

"Yes, ma'am," he stated emphatically as he started the engine and pulled out of the parking lot. They wound down the circular driveway and headed toward town. "And now I'm warned."

"Exactly. Now are you going to feed me?"

"Next is dinner," he agreed, a gleam of respect in his eyes. He took her hand and raised it to his lips in silent apology.

But the moment his lips touched her hand, all the humor of the moment was gone, replaced by excitement.

Refusing to admit to her desire, Sable snatched back her hand, and sat primly, hands in her lap like a schoolmarm.

"Something wrong?"

"No, nothing."

"Then why the chill?" Joe asked, his voice as smooth as the darkness. "I thought you forgave me."

"I did. I do."

Joe breathed heavily, and the sound hung in the silence between them, creating even more tension.

The restaurant was crowded. People filled the rooms, laughter and conversations spilling around them. Sable felt safe once more. It wasn't Joe she didn't trust. It was herself.

They went into the bar to await their table, and once again Sable realized that she thoroughly enjoyed his company. Joe seemed more relaxed, too. In fact, looking back over their short relationship, she didn't think she'd ever seen him this open and easygoing.

"And then, at the ripe old age of twenty-four, I discovered horses. I read countless books on the subject. I rode more than two hundred horses before I finally chose Aruba."

"Aruba?" Sable frowned. She thought she knew the names of all the horses in the barn, but that one didn't sound familiar.

He nodded. "She was a mare with foal, and I loved her the moment I saw her. Two of my horses are hers, a mare and a stallion. She died last year of an overstressed heart. But she was my beginning."

"Most females are," Sable said dryly, aware that there was a twinkle in her eyes.

Joe chuckled. "They're also usually the end."

"Of a good relationship?"

"Of adolescence. Until a boy meets his first woman, he's just a kid."

Sable blushed, and Joe had the audacity to laugh.

"I'm sorry," he said. "I just can't help it. I enjoy getting a rise out of you."

"You enjoy making me feel . . . inadequate."

"No," he corrected softly. "I enjoy watching you blush." He reached out to touch her hand, but withdrew his own at the last moment. "I'm not the perfect gentleman. Hell, half the time I forget my manners entirely. But that's what comes from being around just men for most of my life. There was no sweet-smelling mama to teach me the finer things in life."

"Everybody has a mother."

He nodded, staring into his drink. "And I'm sure I had one, too. But instead of looking at me and deciding to treasure me for the rest of my life, she dropped me into the nearest trash container in Austin, then went blithely on her way. I was raised in a welfare home most of my life, but they didn't take me because I was sweet, either. Harold and Gladys had five children to raise, and I was a little extra money in their pockets."

This time it was Sable who reached across the table, her slight hand covering his. "I'm sorry."

His gaze held hers. "Don't be. I'm not one to complain much about fate. But maybe if I hadn't been raised that way, I wouldn't be where I am today."

She smiled. "You have a point. But no little boy or girl should be without a mother. Have you ever thought of looking for her?"

"When I was young I thought about it a lot. She would find me and be so sorry. She'd cry and beg my forgiveness. And I was going to be a gentleman and do just that. But as I got older it dawned on me that she was probably a young, scared student who didn't know what to do and panicked. Austin has more students than any other city in Texas. None of them seem to be prepared for life, let alone being on their own. I imagine it was tough over thirty years ago. Especially on a woman."

It hurt to think he had no family, no one who cared. "Do you ever see the people who raised you?"

"No. I was just one in a long line of welfare kids for them, and since my middle name was Trouble, I think they were relieved to see me go."

"How long did you live with them?"

"Until I was sixteen. Then I split. One year later I joined the army and saw the world," he said, his voice suddenly filled with sarcasm.

She closed her eyes, imagining being alone during her growing years and knowing the hardship it would have entailed. The thought brought tears to her eyes. "I'm so sorry. No one deserves such a childhood."

"I didn't tell you to gain your sympathy."

"I know."

Their hands intertwined. Sable blinked rapidly to keep the tears at bay. But she couldn't seem to keep out her compassion. She stared down at their hands, then closed her eyes once more.

Joe leaned forward and kissed each eyelid.

"Thank you." His voice was low.

She opened her eyes and smiled through the tears. "You're welcome," she answered.

IT WAS long past eleven when they reached the turnoff to the house. Conversation had flowed so easily and readily at the restaurant that neither had wanted to call an end to the evening. Sable had had three glasses of wine, and that was nice, too.

"Not too much nor too little."

"Too much nor too little of what?" Joe whispered into her ear. That wasn't hard, since her head rested on his shoulder. He was so comfortable. . . .

"Wine."

He chuckled. "Just right," he observed.

She lifted her head and stared at the firm lips shadowed in the dash lights. "What's just right?"

"You are."

She smiled, burrowing her head back into the solidness of his shoulder. "Mmm."

He pulled the car up to the back door and flipped off the ignition. The silence was as relaxing as the drive had been. His head rested against hers and she moved her cheek back and forth, loving the feel of his stubbleroughened chin. Men and women had so many intriguing differences.

Unwilling to put her feelings into words, Sable lifted her face to his. She followed the thick arch of his brow with a fingernail and marveled at the texture. The pad of her forefinger felt the pulse at his temple, amazing her how alive his skin felt. He was beautiful.

She could sense the leashed strength and, like Pandora with her box, she was tempted by it. To open it up, go wild. . . .

She parted her lips.

Joe groaned, and his lips covered hers in a kiss that sought and seared her very soul. His mouth was hungry, moving over hers as if she were the very substance God had created in order for him to be whole. His every action both terrified and excited her, and she loved it.

His arms enfolded her. Then, turning her body, he pressed her against him. Her breasts were first flattened against the hardness of his chest, then swelled in anticipation of more. The low, purring sound she made in the dark, cozy interior of the cab seemed far away.

She wanted his touch with a craving that drove away all thoughts of possible consequences. She pressed even closer, willing to be absorbed by his heat, his masculinity.

The catch in his breathing echoed around her, adding to her headiness. "I want you." His voice was as soft as a whisper, as rough as pebbles on a streambed. "I want you so badly, I don't think I'd live if you said no."

She took a breath, knowing he was asking for her commitment to their marriage. "I'm not saying no," she admitted. "I want you, too."

His breath sighed from his body. "Then shall we go inside, or would you like to continue this right where we are?"

This was a dream and she wanted it to continue. Just like this. They were alone and no one, nothing could interfere. The truck was like a haven from the house, bunkhouse, horses and the world.

"Here."

He chuckled. "Okay, darling, but we'll have to be pretty agile. Right now I have a steering wheel in my left rib."

She pulled back, her hand stroking his side. "I'm sorry. We'll go inside."

His arms tightened around her, pulling her back to his broad chest. "No. We'll stay right here in our own little world." He had understood her reluctance to leave the confines of the cab.

His hand slipped down and hit a button, allowing the seat to glide back as far as it would go.

She smiled in the dark and moved to the flow of his body, loving the feeling. Her lips caressed his chest, pecking light kisses up to his neck and jawline. "You smell so good," she murmured.

"So do you," he answered, but his voice sounded lighter than hers. His hands moved restlessly from her hips to her breasts, then back down again.

He moved her higher against him and stretched his legs the length of the seat. With a soft moan of contentment he kissed her again. Her weight was fully supported on his body, her arms encircling his neck as she gave him kiss for kiss, touch for touch, soft sound for manly harsh groan.

After undoing the buttons of her blouse, he slipped his hand inside to the soft warmth of her breast, his fingers seeking, then finding, the nipple that awaited his attention.

She pressed her fullness against his palm, loving the texture of the calluses on his hand as he touched her.

With a twist, the front snap of her lace bra was undone, and she was free of the material. Bending his head, his lips teased her nipple into his mouth. It was pure, unadulterated pleasure. It was torture. Even he couldn't stand the torment anymore and enclosed her breast with his tongue.

"You taste so good," he murmured, stealing another kiss from her parted lips. "Like heaven and hell all rolled into one."

"You feel the same way," she whispered, her fingers stroking his jaw and nape. His strength was always a surprise to her. Corded muscles jumped and played with each stroke of his shoulders. "It's wonderful."

"Better. Better than wonderful."

Sable didn't know when he had undone her slacks, but when he touched the juncture of her thighs, her breath caught in her throat at the wonder of it. Every thought fled her mind. Sensation after sensation washed over her, and she felt as if she were going to die. She arched her body, following his directions as he settled her closer to his lap. His touch was magic, his fingers stroking her as if he knew her innermost secrets and desires.

She wanted him so much! Realizing she was unprotected, she mentally flipped through the calendar of the past month. She should be safe right now.

She reached between them to touch him the same way, but Joe stopped her. "Easy, darling," he murmured, his breath warm on her temple. "Soon," he promised. "Soon."

When he finally entered her, it was as if they'd been born to fit that way. He thrust and she clung to his broad shoulders. He was the only thing anchoring her to the earth. Her breathing was short, matching his as they exchanged kisses. Her mind was numb, overwhelmed by a flood of emotions. She'd never felt—never responded—this way before, and his every move sent her closer and closer to the edge. It was frightening. It was wonderful. Ecstasy began immediately, filling her with more love for him than she'd ever thought herself capable of.

She felt him clench his muscles and knew he was feeling the same thrill she was, and her surprised and delighted laughter filled the air.

Joe's arms tightened, then he moved her against him for a final time, and her laughter became a moan of incredulous delight.

6

IT WASN'T until the early morning hours that Sable and Joe, arms entwined, strolled through the back door into the house. The moon lighted their way, smiling benignly, as if giving its blessing.

When they reached Joe's bedroom, he turned her toward him and gently teased her mouth with tiny kisses. This time intimate contact took precedence over passion. His stroking hands spoke volumes, telling her that most of all he loved holding her and didn't want to let her go. He made her feel warm, wanted, cared for.

But still unwilling to admit that her feelings matched his, Sable pulled away, then rested her head on his chest. The deep, steady thud of his heartbeat sounded in her ear as she relaxed against him. Closing her eyes, she pretended the moment would last forever. They were both very still for a long, peaceful time.

When at last she looked up, she touched with exquisite gentleness the few strands of gray at his temple, her fingers caressing his pulse points as her heartbeat matched the rhythm of his.

She was still stunned by her reaction to his touch. It was a shock to realize she had such passion imprisoned inside her. And Joe was the one who'd released it.

She brushed her lips against his, savoring the contact. "Good night," she said softly.

Holding her, he leaned against the doorjamb. "You're not going to spend the rest of the night with me?"

Not trusting her voice, Sable shook her head.

"Why not?"

"Give me time," she finally pleaded, ignoring her own reluctance to leave him. How could she say that she couldn't think clearly around him? She needed to sort through her emotions. Right now she felt both wonderful and frightened. And she wasn't capable of making a decision. Any decision. Besides, it just didn't seem right to let those in her world know what had happened this night. Not yet. She needed time to realize it herself. "This has all happened so quickly."

"It doesn't make sense," he whispered in a deep, growling tone. "We can't just ignore what happened between us." He threaded his fingers through her hair, framing her face with his hands. His blue eyes locked with hers. "And it *did* happen."

She understood, but his presence left her no room to think things through. "Please," she begged, curling her hand on his chest. "Don't rush."

Joe took a step back, and her hand dropped to the space left between them. His eyes narrowed, taking in her pale face. Violet circles rimmed her eyes, visible even in the dim light of dawn. She was exhausted and probably a little confused. And so was he.

"Okay." He sighed. "Just this time."

"Thank you." She kissed the tip of his chin.

"Sleep well."

She smiled. "I'll try."

NO RISK, NO OBLIGATION TO BUY...NOW OR EVER!

GUARANTEED

PLAY "ROLL A DOUBLE" AND GET AS MANY AS SIX GIFTS!

HERE'S HOW TO PLAY:

1. Peel off label from front cover.Place it in space provided at right.With a coin, carefully scratch off the silver dice.This makes you eligible to receive one or more free books, and possibly other gifts, depending on what is revealed beneath the scratch-off area.

2. You'll receive brand-new Harlequin Temptation® novels. When you return this card, we'll rush you the books and gifts you qualify for ABSOLUTELY FREE!

3. Then, if we don't hear from you, every month we'll send you 4 additional novels to read and enjoy. You can return them and owe nothing, but if you decide to keep them, you'll pay only $2.39* per book - a savings of 26¢ each off the cover price.And, there's no extra charge for postage and handling!

4. When you subscribe to the Harlequin Reader Service®, you'll also get our newsletter, as well as additional free gifts from time to time.

5. You must be completely satisfied.You may cancel at any time simply by sending us a note or a shipping statement marked "cancel" or by returning any shipment to us at our expense.

You'll love your elegant 20K gold electroplated chain! The necklace is finely crafted with 160 double-soldered links, and is electroplate finished in genuine 20K gold. And it's yours FREE as an added thanks for giving our Reader Service a try!

"ROLL A DOUBLE!"

PLACE LABEL HERE

?

SCRATCH HERE

SEE CLAIM CHART BELOW

142 CIH MDWE
(U-H-T-09/90)

YES! I have placed my label from the front cover into the space provided above and scratched off the silver dice. Please rush me the free book(s) and gift(s) that I am entitled to. I understand that I am under no obligation to purchase any books, as explained on the opposite page.

NAME

ADDRESS   APT.

CITY   STATE   ZIP CODE

CLAIM CHART

⚃ ⚃	**4 FREE BOOKS PLUS FREE 20k ELECTROPLATED GOLD CHAIN PLUS MYSTERY BONUS GIFT**	
⚁ ⚄	**3 FREE BOOKS PLUS BONUS GIFT**	
⚅ ⚂	**2 FREE BOOKS**	

CLAIM NO.37-829

HARLEQUIN "NO RISK" GUARANTEE
- You're not required to buy a single book - ever!
- You must be completely satisfied or you may cancel at any time simply by sending us a note or a shipping statement marked "cancel" or by returning any shipment to us at our cost. Either way, you will receive no more books; you'll have no further obligation.
- The free book(s) and gift(s) you claimed on this "Roll A Double" offer remain yours to keep no matter what you decide.

His kiss on her forehead was slow and sweet, sealing their earlier actions. She pulled away and walked toward her room across the hall.

Joe backed into his own room and softly closed the door.

Undressing in the moonlight, Sable mulled over potential problems they might have created during these past wonderful hours. But her thoughts still couldn't focus on them. Everything was too new and shiny, and her emotions were too jumbled.

She slipped between the cool sheets, believing she would be awake for what remained of the night. Instead her eyes closed almost instantly and she fell into a deep slumber.

JOE TOSSED his pants and shirt into a corner and got into bed. But his eyes refused to close. The bed was too empty, the room too cold. Moonlight was dimming outside his window, but he wasn't ready for the new day.

There was only one solution to all his problems: Sable.

An hour later, the answer was still Sable.

Joe slipped from the bed and reached for his robe. He slung it over his arm, opened the door and listened to make sure the kids were still sleeping. Then he walked across the hall to Sable's room and slowly twisted the knob.

Standing at the foot of the bed, he gazed. She was asleep, curled in a small knot on one side of the bed. Against her back, where Joe should have been, was a pillow. She looked vulnerable, contented and... beautiful.

The deep well of tenderness he felt as he stared at her took him by surprise. It was more than lust. It was more than loneliness. Shaking his head, he refused to label it. But it scared the hell out of him.

He couldn't resist. He walked stealthily around the side of the bed and slipped between the sheets. Carefully he moved the pillow from her back and replaced it with his own body. Edging his knee between hers, he rested one arm on the slim curve of her waist. She wriggled closer; the imprint of her body against him was heaven. Sighing contentedly, he closed his eyes. With her body nestled in his arms, he slept at last.

TALIA'S VOICE ripped through Sable's dream.

"Sable, we've overslept!" she cried, opening the bedroom door. "It's after nine, and I'm supposed to be at cheerleader tryouts—"

Sable stirred. It was so very cosy here in her bed. A small, satisfied sound echoed in her throat, and she snuggled closer to the welcome warmth. Perhaps, if she didn't open her eyes, Talia would disappear.

A male chuckle resounded in her ear and sent a shiver down her spine. A soft breath touched her temple. The weight that felt so good on her waist moved. Her body grew rigid. She had to be wrong. She must be wrong. Cautiously she straightened her leg, only to encounter someone else's flesh. Muscled flesh. Talia's giggle told her she was right. Joe was in bed with her.

And apparently as stark naked as she was.

Her first reaction was to flee. Sable rolled away and sat up, clutching the sheet to her bosom like an outraged spinster. Totally ignoring the goggle-eyed teenager, she turned to Joe. "What are you doing here?" she demanded.

Talia giggled again.

Joe grinned. "Sleeping."

"But you're not supposed to be sleeping here!"

"Well, not anymore today," he agreed evenly. "Now I'm going to get up and go to work. We overslept, as Talia so kindly informed us."

She glanced over her shoulder at the teenager. "Talia, leave, please." Then she turned to Joe once more. "I mean you shouldn't be here!"

He raised his brows. "Why not? It is legal, you know. I'm your husband."

"I know! But—" she began.

Sable's gaze darted back to her young sister. Behind her stood Jonathan, his eyes button bright as he looked with undeniable interest from his hero to his mama.

"Mommy like Joe?" the little boy asked.

Sable couldn't answer that question. Not now. "Talia, take Jonathan and leave, please." Her voice shook with anger. At least she told herself it was anger. She wasn't ready to face being found in bed with the man she'd married in name only. And she wasn't ready for the questions she was sure Jonathan would ask. But most of all she wasn't ready for the commitment this action implied.

Talia looked disappointed. She took the youngster by the hand and slowly moved toward the door. Their eyes remained on the couple in bed.

"Now, Talia," Sable urged.

When the door closed behind them, Sable focused all her anger and frustration on the cause of this problem. "What the hell do you think you're doing in my bed?"

"Sleeping," was his prompt reply.

"You were supposed to sleep in your own bed. You agreed," she said, trying to fill her voice with grit.

Head tilted to one side, he stared as though examining her for some rare disease. "I know, but I changed my mind. Is something going on in that tousled head of yours that I don't know about?" he asked quietly.

"Don't try to avoid the issue." Sable bit out each word. "You weren't supposed to come in here, and I want you out. Now."

His eyes narrowed. "You mean I'm good enough to make love to in the cab of a truck, but I'm not good enough to take to bed?" Obviously his patience was ending, too. "What am I? A yard dog with fleas? Good enough to play fetch outside, but not good enough to bring into the house?"

"Of course not!" She took a deep breath to calm the quaking that seemed to permeate her body. "But you promised I'd have time to think this through! Then you climb into my bed and announce to my family that we're sleeping together, without bothering to think how I'd feel about telling them."

"We're married."

"I know." She pulled at the sheet, wrapping it around herself as she stood. She needed to get away. "But this wasn't the way it was supposed to happen. My son shouldn't have to find a man in my bed without my explaining all this to him."

"Why not? We're not strangers."

"Don't start with me, Joe Lombardi!" Sable took another step backward. "You were supposed to stay in your own bed...your own room, until we worked this out. Our contract stipulated that you and I maintain separate bedrooms and all that that entails. I want to keep it that way." She pushed back an errant strand of hair and glared at him. He had no right to look so calm, as if this happened every day.

Apparently oblivious to his own nudity, Joe let the blanket fall away and got up, his tanned form beautifully outlined by the sun from the window. "Correction. You were the one who needed to work things out. I know what I want." His voice was hard, his features carved in granite.

"And just what was it you want, Joe?" she asked sarcastically. "Sex? A little fooling around before you leave for a hard day's work?"

Joe surprised her by nodding his head. "Yes," he answered. "But that's not all. I also want a little stroking. You know, some of the comforting things a *wife* does."

She didn't miss the mingled hurt and sarcasm in his voice. And for just a second she felt she'd let him down. But the feeling led to defensiveness. "You want sex, plain and simple."

"I haven't denied it. But as I said, that's not all I want."

"Get out," Sable ordered, suddenly unable to continue this conversation. If she'd been confused last night, it was nothing compared to now. Her chin tilted upward, warning that she was ready for battle.

"But throw something on first," she said coldly. "Remember there are others in this house."

His face mirrored his frustration as Joe took a threatening step toward her, but he stopped at the end of the bed. "Forget it," he said disgustedly, reaching for his robe. "You have some pretty deep-seated problems, lady. You're right. I shouldn't have come in here and tried to extend our wonderful time in the truck. I thought you were an adult as well as my wife. You're the person I should be thrilled to live with in wedded bliss. As you've just proven, you're not worth the aggravation or the trouble."

Joe opened the door. "Call me when you have your act together. Maybe, if I'm still around, I'll consider an apology."

It was her fault. Their lovemaking had ended in warfare.

One phrase had really hit home. *The person I should be thrilled to live with in wedded bliss!*

Since her marriage she'd thought only of the sacrifices she'd made for her son and sister. She had chosen her way of life, then found a man to help her do exactly what she wanted. But she'd given no thought to Joe's sacrifices, his personal needs, his life-style.

For the next five years he'd given up the right to be seen in public with other women.

He couldn't even think of having a relationship with a woman.

Because of this marriage, he'd probably never have children of his own. By the time they got divorced and he found a woman to love, he could conceivably be in his forties and decided the time for fatherhood had passed him by. Then all that joy would never be experienced.

He'd lost his freedom and, in his own home, he'd lost his privacy.

He received a million dollars for giving up those rights! a little voice argued.

They'd both been dumb.

It had been easy to sit in an attorney's office and spout off living conditions. After the wedding they'd learned the difficulty of living up to rules and regulations written in ignorance. And as time went on, the stress of their day-to-day married lives had worsened.

Until last night.

Guilt hit her hard.

And so did memories of last night.

Joe had been so attentive all evening that Sable had let her guard down. By the time he kissed her, she'd been ready to ignore the small voice inside, telling her to slow down.

Now, clutching the sheet still wrapped around her like a Grecian robe, Sable sat on the edge of the bed.

She should have seen where this was leading, instead of just riding the crest of the wave of sensuality. But it had been so new, so incredible. So overwhelming. Joe's touch had lured her into an uncharted land.

It was all her fault. Maybe if she'd treated the whole episode as lightly as he had, no one, including little Johnny, would have thought anything unusual about it. But she'd blown it all out of proportion.

After firmly telling Talia that she would have nothing to do with the man on a physical level, she'd been embarrassed to be found with him in her bed. That knowing look in Talia's eyes had turned her embarrassment into anger and she had exploded at Joe, instead of the real culprit: herself.

JOE CURSED LOUDLY in the shower stall. He'd made a perfectly sane decision to court Sable. He had planned to show her just how gentlemanly he could be. How considerate. In fact, he'd shown her what a jackass he could be.

He wasn't sure what kind of relationship she'd had with John, and wasn't certain he wanted to know. But he had realized that, for a married woman, Sable was very innocent when it came to acknowledging her own sensuality. Yet she had responded with openness and passion he'd never thought he'd find, making their lovemaking all the more incredible. That should have given him a clue as to her confusion, had he thought about it for even a minute.

Instead he'd crawled into her bed. He'd ruined the whole damn thing by forcing her into an open relationship, before she had absorbed all the changes. He'd forced her into displaying their attraction to her family, when she hadn't even admitted it to herself.

He'd rushed her.

He'd fumbled it.

Another muttered curse rang off the tiled shower walls.

But the worst sin, he told himself, was that he didn't know what to do next. He'd lost his temper this morning and said things he didn't mean. But his ego had been pretty bruised. He'd reacted out of instinct, lashing out at her, rather than thinking things through and trying to salvage something from the chaos.

He owed her an apology. But something told him that spitting in his face would give her greater pleasure right now.

Stepping out of the shower, he dried off and stepped into his work clothes.

He had faced the jungles of the Vietcong. He had fought off thugs in a dimly lighted parking lot. He could stare down an irate banker at ten paces. But he was going to run away from one small female who was even more vulnerable than she was feisty.

Replacing the hairbrush on his dresser, he stared at the man in the mirror. "Sounds safe to me." The words echoed defeatedly around the room.

SABLE REHEARSED several apologies but she never had a chance to speak to Joe, because he avoided her. He came in after midnight every night and was gone before seven in the morning.

"I don't see what's so wrong about the situation." Talia's voice startled Sable as she wound the cord on the vacuum cleaner.

"What situation?"

"You know," Talia drawled, dropping into a plush, upholstered chair. "Between you and Joe."

"It's none of your business." Sable couldn't count the times she'd said that in the past week.

"Well, I still don't see anything wrong with it."

"I'll pretend you never said anything, so I won't have to be angry. But one more word of warning, Talia.

Please don't bring this issue up again. I just want to forget it."

"Boy!" Talia exclaimed. "You tell me to be strong, make decisions, accept what mistakes you make and go on! Maybe you should follow your own advice."

With as much dignity as she could muster, Sable ignored Talia's last comment and left the room, wishing her thoughts could be left behind as easily.

She decided the kitchen needed a thorough cleaning. Jonathan was napping and the house was quiet. The only way to occupy her mind was to keep busy.

She glanced at the note on the table, then focused on the sink full of dishes. She knew the note—all Joe's notes—by heart. They had been communicating all week by notes left on the kitchen table. She wrote her answers to the messages written in the morning and left them on the table for him to find at night.

She filled the sink with sudsy water and sighed. Maybe washing the dishes by hand would take her mind off Joe. The whole situation would be comical if she didn't feel the way she did about the man.

She loved Joe. She loved him so much, she was afraid of his rejection. So instead of approaching her husband and telling him she cared for him, she avoided him. Just as he avoided her.

Tears filled her eyes, and she tried to blink them away. Every time she remembered the passion they had shared, she wanted more—so much more.

She wanted Joe to feel the same way she did. She wanted him to stride in the door, take her into his arms and kiss her until she swooned. Was that too much to ask? Yes! came the resounding answer.

Despite her efforts to forget it, there was the issue of the money. He wouldn't have had the chance to make love to her if she hadn't bought him. He'd still be free and single and probably making love to some other lucky woman. And Sable would have never known just what she was missing.

She had to do something!

She'd give Joe some time to make the first move, but if, by this time next week, nothing had happened, she would approach Joe, kiss him, then apologize.

Maybe he would take the initiative. She straightened her shoulders. It didn't matter. She'd made the decision. She would hold herself to it.

SEVEN DRAGGING DAYS PASSED, and Joe still made no move in her direction. He continued to stay out of her way.

On the afternoon of her self-imposed deadline she took Jonathan to the barn, and they mucked out the horses' stalls.

By the time they'd finished, she was hot and tired and sweaty. "Okay," she told the horses. "You've been given the equivalent of clean sheets, and I don't have to worry about you for another week." She wiped her hands on her jeans.

Johnny stood in a ray of sunshine, chubby hands wrapped around the handle of the rake as he smiled up at her. Suddenly all was almost right with her world.

"Oh, you think that's funny, do you?" she teased.

Johnny nodded. "Horses don't talk, Mommy."

"Well, some do! They just wait till we're not around, then they tell stories about how funny we humans are."

Johnny shook his head. "No."

The sound of boots hitting concrete caught her attention. Her hand still on the boy's shoulder, Sable turned.

Joe strode toward them. His hair was damp. His shirt clung to broad shoulders, chest and arms. His blue eyes were narrowed, focused on her. She felt like a butterfly caught on a pin.

Joe halted in front of her and stared down.

Her heart beat frantically in her breast. "Hi." Her voice was a whisper.

"Hi, beautiful." Wrapping his arms about her, he pulled her close to the lean hardness of his body. When his head came down and his lips claimed hers, she responded instantly. Heartbeat quickening, she curled her arms around his neck and clung to the strength of him. His mouth, hard, possessive, breathtaking, answered with the same fervor. A soft sound came from somewhere. It didn't register at first that she'd made it.

When the kiss ended, she felt bereft. He placed her head against the solidness of his chest, and his lips grazed her ear. "I'm sorry," he murmured into her hair. "I didn't mean to hurt you."

"I'm sorry, too." Relief flooded her, soothing away her worries. Joe had apologized to her!

"And we have company."

"Here?"

He nodded. But it wasn't until he turned to one side and pulled away that she saw two figures on the threshold. Then Jonathan gave a happy cry, dropped his rake and ran toward them.

Sable and Joe turned to face the visitors together.

Her heart sank.

Jonathan's grandparents stood there, rigid and uncertain, awaiting recognition.

With his arm about her waist, Joe guided Sable toward them. Still dazed, it took her a moment to bid the pair a cool welcome.

How could they face her, when they'd written such an awful letter just weeks ago, demanding she give them Jonathan? How could Joe act so cordially, so hospitably to the people who wanted to tear her family apart? If only she'd told him about the letter. Once more she'd fouled up by not telling him everything.

But Jonathan clearly had no reservations. He was in his grandfather's arms, hugging him as fervently as Sable had hugged Joe.

"We just wanted to see Jonathan," Mrs. LaCroix said with a catch in her throat.

Sable stared at her, their eyes meeting and warring. The older woman looked away first, and Sable realized that she had won. John's parents would never have come here if they hadn't been told they could not win custody of Jonathan.

For a moment Sable felt sorry for the exquisitely dressed older woman. All the money in the world wouldn't bring her son back. It couldn't even buy visitation rights to her grandson.

"We're glad you came," Sable replied. "This is my husband, Joe Lombardi. He and John were friends."

Joe nodded at the woman and held out his hand to John's father.

"Where did you know my son?" the older man questioned.

"Nam. We were foxhole buddies," Joe explained.

Sable slipped her hand through Joe's bent arm. "Come inside. Iced tea should help stave off this August heat."

Jonathan was still in his grandfather's arms when Sable and Joe led the couple into the living room.

Quickly Sable went to the kitchen and made the tea. She added sprigs of fresh mint to the glasses, then placed them on a tray with the sugar. After a moment's hesitation, she decided to leave everything exactly as it was. After all, she lived a simple life now. No silver or crystal.

And Joe was Joe. It didn't really matter whether John's parents liked him or not. They were no longer her in-laws. They were just Jonathan's grandparents.

Taking a deep breath, Sable picked up the tray and walked to the living room.

Joe was sitting cross-legged on the floor. Jonathan, wrapped around his back, giggled as he tickled his stepfather's neck.

The LaCroix looked on.

"He's quite a guy," Joe commented to André La-Croix.

"I agree." The expression on the older man's face reflected his pride. Sable knew that, though there was little resemblance between Jonathan and his father, André saw his son in his grandson.

"Here it is," Sable said, forcing a cheery note into her voice. She placed the tray on the coffee table.

Suddenly thoughtful, she watched everyone. Had she made such a fuss about the big, bad LaCroix that she'd blown the whole situation out of proportion? She didn't think so. Anyone who tried to take away a child from his parent to be raised by hired help was untrustworthy. And that letter *had* been a threat.

"Where's your sister?" Mrs. LaCroix asked. "I thought she lived with you."

"She does," Sable said, choosing her words carefully. "She's finishing her school supply shopping."

"So you're still raising her."

"She's still living with me, yes," Sable amended. Talia had always been too outspoken for the LaCroix to enjoy.

Arms outstretched, Johnny came to Sable. "Drink, please," he said as he climbed into her lap. Proud that he remembered his manners in front of his grandparents, she kissed the tip on his nose and tickled his stomach.

He gave an endearing grin. With a tender smile she allowed him a sip of her tea.

"You look very well," Mrs. LaCroix said softly.

Sable's surprised gaze darted to the older woman. "Thank you. I'm happy."

"I can see that. And so is Jonathan."

Sable nodded. "Jonathan's always happy as long as he has his way," she answered.

"Don't I know it! His father was the same way, always smiling as long as I gave him what he wanted...." Her voice faded; she'd evidently realized she was speaking of Sable's first husband in the presence of the new one. "Oh, I'm sorry!" she exclaimed, holding one hand to her cheek in dismay. "I didn't mean to . . ."

"It's okay." Joe's voice was gentle, but firm. "John was my friend, too. And I want Jonathan to know about his father."

Sable could have kissed Joe when she saw relief in the expressions of her former in-laws. Without Joe to defuse some of the initial awkwardness, this visit would have been disastrous.

The rest of the visit was calm, without the usual tension Sable felt with the LaCroix. In fact, she was surprised to find it a pleasant visit.

They walked the older couple out to the driveway. Mr. LaCroix stood uncertainly at the side of the car. "We only want to see our grandson."

"And you can." Sable knew her smile was forced, but she meant the words. "But I can't allow you to spoil him rotten. Children need strong guidelines and a lot of love."

"May we visit again soon?" the older man asked, his hand outstretched toward Joe.

"Anytime," Joe told him, before Sable could answer.

As they drove away, Joe stood with one arm holding Jonathan, the other around Sable. The older couple waved goodbye and the car disappeared into the distance. Still holding her firmly, Joe turned and directed Sable up the porch steps.

Jonathan ran into the house and off to his room to play.

Sable looked up at Joe, marveling at the strength and gentleness he always displayed. "Thank you," she said softly.

"Nothing to it," he muttered, suddenly embarrassed.

She placed her hand on his arm. "Yes, there was. And I thank you for making it easier."

His eyes narrowed as he looked at her for the first time since the LaCroix had left. "Sable, why did you marry me?"

Her eyes widened. "So I could keep Jonathan. You knew that."

"No," he declared quickly. "I mean the real reason. What was it? Did you like being married? Or did you want your own home, without the bother of battling your way out of theirs?"

Sable wrinkled her brow in puzzlement. "The threat of Jonathan's grandparents fighting for custody *is* the real reason."

"That's an excuse, Sable." His voice hardened. "Those people might think about taking Jonathan, but only if their grandparental rights were threatened. As long as you didn't keep them from seeing their grandson, there wouldn't be a problem."

So that was it. He'd taken them at face value. And she hadn't helped any by not telling him about the letter. "You're wrong," she told him firmly. "I know them. I heard their attorney try to reason with them, but they wanted custody. They were willing to fight for it. In court."

Joe opened his mouth, but she held up her hand to stop him. "And just two short weeks ago they wrote another letter, telling me they wanted to raise my son and send him away to school. Those people mean business when they speak or act, Joe. And I know a challenge when I see one."

Joe shook his head. "Maybe, but I don't think so. I think they just wanted the right to see their grandson, and were afraid you were taking that right away. That's all."

Her hands shook so hard, she placed them on her hips. "You don't know them. You weren't there. I was."

"And you panicked. In your rush to ensure custody of Jonathan, you offered me a million dollars for a marriage you didn't need and obviously don't want." His voice was sad and heavy.

"And you agreed."

"No," he corrected. "I agreed to marry you. I don't believe that they were trying to take away your child."

Frustration filled her. "What do you care? Jonathan's not your responsibility. You never stayed up with him at night, watched him cut his first tooth or cried when he fell and hurt himself. You weren't there. I was."

"And if you had your way, I think you'd like to keep Jonathan away from me, too, Sable. You'd love to have him all to yourself, with no one else to claim his attention. That's not right, for you or for Jonathan." Joe's voice still sounded as tired and defeated as he looked.

He walked inside, then stopped and looked back at her. "Though you didn't have to marry me, you did. Now you'll have to make the best of it. Because this is all we have."

"And you?" she asked, trying to read his expression. "Why did you marry me?"

"One reason was money," he admitted in a tone of finality. He turned and headed toward the back door.

"I'll be at the track," he said over his shoulder and left the house.

"Wait!" she called, running after him.

But the truck was pulling away as she ran down the back steps.

Fists clenched at her sides, she watched him drive around the house and toward the road. "We're not through yet, Joe Lombardi," she muttered. "Not by a long shot."

7

SCHOOL BEGAN, and Talia was caught up in the hectic process of making friends and settling into classes. Talia had a talent for fitting in and getting whatever she wanted. She'd already passed the cheerleading tests. Sable had helped her sister develop her self-confidence because she was aware of how sorely she lacked it herself.

Now she even doubted she was capable of gaining Joe's attention by being a wonderful wife and mother. It would be so much easier to just give up. But a small, inner voice told her to believe in herself, and so she continued to try.

These days Sable hardly saw Joe and when she did, he was distant and preoccupied. She knew he was fighting both a deadline and the Texas Racing Commission.

Because gambling was to be legal for the first time since the turn of the century, every detail of policy had to be carefully evaluated. Whatever the board did, they checked with other state commissions first, to see the process before setting up their own. And all of it created more paperwork and headaches for Joe.

Sable prepared gourmet meals, but Joe never came home to eat. Exasperated, she decided at last that she'd go to him.

She dressed with great care and standing before the mirror, decided the effort had been worthwhile. Her long hair swung about her shoulders and her makeup was flawless. Outwardly she appeared cool and assured, but inside she quivered.

Resolutely she marched into the kitchen and placed her husband's hot meal in a plastic container.

At least he'll eat one of my meals, she thought grimly.

Leaving Talia to watch Jonathan and to do her homework, Sable drove toward the racetrack. This would be her first visit to the track and the closer she came, the guiltier she felt. After all, they had been married over a month. She should have shown more interest in what was her husband's consuming passion—what kept him away from her.

The road to the stadium was lined with tall pines, and late-afternoon sunlight sent dappled shadows across the double-lane road. Entering the grounds, she gasped in surprise when she saw the huge building.

The structure could have been taken from a 1940s romantic movie set. A five-story, stucco building, ornately balustraded, rose through the trees. Walls in a rich cream and carved, dark wood balconies were interspersed with enormous, floor-to-ceiling windows, perfect foils for the brown bark and forest-green background of towering pines.

A row of booths for ticket takers and valet parking attendants flanked broad, semicircular steps leading up to the wide front entrance.

Sable let the car coast to a slow stop. When she turned off the ignition, the droning noise of a saw and the intermittent sound of a hammer echoed hollowly in the distance.

Holding the plastic dish as if it were a talisman, she stepped outside, then wondered what to do next. Her first impulse was to get into the car again and drive off. A home-cooked meal seemed a flimsy excuse to interfere with a project as big as this one.

Just as she was about to retreat, she heard a shout. "Hey, boss! You got company!"

Looking up, she saw a workman standing on one of the side roofs, as if he had all the world under his control. It took her a moment to realize that the man holding the hammer was her husband.

She waved weakly.

Joe didn't return her greeting. Instead he turned, walked up the roof and disappeared over the edge.

Now what should she do? Wait? Disappear? Pretend she hadn't seen his rebuff? Her heart pounded. She was filled with indecision. Then she spied him, hammer still in hand, walking toward her through the enormous lobby. The sound of his heavy boots rang through the building. When he reached the top of the shallow steps, he stopped. His plaid shirt was tucked securely into old, body-hugging jeans, but the day's heat had obviously forced him to unbutton his shirt. He looked gorgeous.

"Is everything all right?" he called.

Sable nodded, then cleared her throat. "Yes. I just brought you something to eat."

His brows rose. "Come on up."

The command held no note of anger, so she did his bidding.

As she reached his side, she stopped, hands still clutching the dish. "This building is beautiful!" Her awestruck tone added emphasis to her words.

"Yes," he agreed quietly, his dark eyes resting on her face.

Sable raised a hand to her cheek. "Is my makeup smeared?"

His grin was slow and easy. It drew her like a magnet. He took her arm and escorted her through the impressive entrance doors, adjusting his longer step to the cadence of hers. "Your makeup is perfect. Let's go into the office, where I can see what you've brought me."

Just inside the lobby was a bank of elevators. Joe ushered her in and, without taking his eyes from her, pushed the button for the fifth floor. His smile was still turning up the corners of his lips.

Now she became even more nervous. "What's the completion date?"

He shrugged. "If I win, it's a month from tomorrow. If the racing commission wins, it's within two weeks."

"And what are the chances of the commission winning?"

"Fifty-fifty," he muttered, still holding her arm as the elevator doors opened.

They stepped out and he ushered her down an area that apparently would become a large, glassed-in gallery facing the track. She was enthralled with the view.

A wide track encircled an oval of green lawn. Within its boundaries was a beautifully landscaped pond. Swans and ducks glided over mirrorlike water and paraded up and down grassy knolls created especially for them.

"The track is finished!" Sable exclaimed in surprise.

"Yes. So are the barns, quarters and most of the offices. The parking lots and the building itself are all that's left. A personnel company in Conroe is hiring the employees now."

"Oh?" Her eyes darted around the complex, straying here and there even as he led her to another door. "How many do you need?"

"About a thousand."

They entered a large office with the same enchanting view as the gallery beyond.

"A thousand people?" she asked incredulously.

"Yes. One thousand," he repeated gently.

"But what will a thousand people do?"

"Some will be trained to place the bets and calculate payoffs on computers. Others will keep the grounds up, work in the restaurants, the bars, the office or the stable."

He took the plastic-covered dish from her and placed it on the desk. "What's this?"

"Swiss Bliss," she said absently, still staring at him.

How could he be so calm, knowing he had to hire a thousand people in less than a month? Knowing he had to have a payroll for that many people?

"What's Swiss Bliss?"

"It's meat, potatoes, carrots, onions and tomatoes, all baked together with assorted spices," she answered distractedly.

"It looks delicious. Did you bring a fork?" Dipping his finger into the tomato and onion gravy, he tasted it.

"Oh, yes." She reached into her purse and pulled out napkin-wrapped utensils. Her mind whirled. How could she not have known what a huge operation this was to be? "Can you manage that large a payroll?"

He nodded, then took his first mouthful of the meal she'd cooked. "If we don't have any more problems. The first race will help us out there."

Her glance was wary. A thousand-person payroll was a large amount of money. "When is the first race?"

"When we open."

"But you're not sure when you open."

Realizing she wouldn't be happy until all her questions were answered, Joe began explaining. "The first race is one month away. That's why I don't want to open until then. Two nights before the race we'll have the grand opening. A catering firm in Dallas has been handling those arrangements for the past several weeks. If the commission insists, I can open in two weeks, but I want the extra time to train the workers and work the bugs out of the computer equipment."

"Oh." She tried to pretend that it made sense. "But if the first race is a month away, why does the racing commission want you to open earlier?"

"Because, since they're not sure what they're doing, they need the time to teach their men. They want the government men to be established before racing starts."

"What government men?"

Joe sighed, then patiently continued. "Racing committee policies are set by the director of racing. Three men are racing stewards. Two represent the track before the racing commission and one represents the state. Then there are the IRS men who must be available, in case someone wins big. Uncle Sam gets his cut off the top."

"I didn't know," she said, shocked by how little thought she'd given to his work. She'd only been to a racetrack once, during the first year she and John were married. "Will they give you any leeway on the time dispute?"

"If Mike is the crackerjack attorney I think he is, the answer is yes."

"I see."

She watched Joe enjoy his lunch. At least there was something she could do right, even if it was only cooking a meal for her man. *Her man.* What an obsolete expression! And she loved it.

"Delicious," he commented. "And spicy," he added.

"I always make it spicy. It's the best way."

He leaned back in the plush, leather chair. "Only if you don't have an ulcer."

That startled her. "Do you have one?"

He nodded. "Uh-huh."

"Why didn't you tell me?"

"Because you were so busy hating me. I was afraid that if you found out, you might make your meals even spicier," he admitted ruefully.

She shook her head. And she had thought there was one thing she was doing right! "I'll grant you that I'm opinionated on occasion, Joe. But I'm not vindictive."

"I know that now." He scooted his chair back. "Come here," he said, patting his leg.

Sable's heart lightened. For the first time in weeks, Joe was relaxed and happy. She'd missed him.

Sorely tempted to do as he asked, she was nonetheless unwilling to look too eager. "I came here on a mission of mercy. I didn't come for hanky-panky," she lied.

"This will be a mission of mercy," he promised. "Come here. Please."

That did the trick. Cautiously she perched on his lap, her back straight, hands resting stiffly on his shoulders.

"There, that's better," he murmured, laying his head against the softness of her breast. His sigh penetrated her soul. The masculine scent of him rose to her nostrils, and she took a deep breath.

But still wary, Sable held her breath, waiting for his next move. She wanted to run her fingers through his springy, dark hair. His warm breath penetrated her light blouse, touching her skin as surely as if it had been his hand.

"You smell so good." His lips touched the curve of her breast, teasing her nipple.

She swallowed. "So do you."

His light clasp at her waist tightened ever so slightly. "And feel so good," he added.

"So do you."

Finally she gave in. Her fingers lost themselves in the thick texture of his hair. She could feel her body relaxing, responding to his closeness.

Joe breathed deeply, his head settling ever closer to the point of her breast. His arms encircled her and his hands, lightly rubbing her back, followed the slender curve of her spine.

She rested her cheek on his head, trying to clear her thoughts and come up with the apology she had composed earlier. Nothing came to mind.

"Sable."

"Hmm?" Her hands seemed to have a will of their own. They wanted to touch the length, breadth and strength of his shoulders, back and neck. He was strong and he smelled like hot sun and fresh earth. He was intoxicating.

"I want more."

"More what?" Her mind was fogged, slow.

"More from our marriage."

Those words got through. The payroll came unbidden to her mind.

She sat up, pulling away from him. "More money?" she asked, her voice thin. This was what she'd always dreaded. Joe had married her for money, so why wouldn't he ask for more? "Are you asking to commingle our assets?"

She saw Joe stare up at her, his blue eyes suddenly narrowed. "Do you really believe that?"

She shook her head. When she was with him, she couldn't believe that money was all he wanted. Only when she was alone did doubts gnaw away at her. "Well, you told me about the payroll and wanting to wait until just before opening."

"And you thought it was an invitation for you to contribute to the cause."

"I don't know. I'm asking you."

Joe's hands slipped down to her waist and tightened their grip. With one smooth movement he helped her stand, then stood himself. His lips brushed hers, leaving her speechless. Was he angry with her? Or was he telling her that he did want the money?

He turned away and began putting the silverware he'd used into the plastic container.

"Thank you for dinner," he said, placing the plastic lid on top. "It was good. Goodbye."

Before she realized what he was about, he was striding through the door. "Joe!" she cried. "Wait!"

"Can't," he called over his shoulder. "There's work to do. Goodbye."

By the time she forced her legs to move to the door, he was in the elevator.

He was gone. Again.

Suddenly anger filled her. "Okay, Lombardi!" she shouted through the empty building. She didn't care who heard, as long as Joe did. "Run away again! That's all you've been doing since we got married!"

The only answer was the faraway whirr of the elevator as it descended to the ground floor.

As silence fell, she became aware of how ridiculous her accusation had been. If he had wanted more money, he wouldn't have insisted on the prenuptial agreement. Nor did he have to play papa to a three-year-old or an older brother to Talia.

Sable didn't understand why, but Joe brought out all her insecurity, the craziness she'd never known she had—until now. Her feelings seesawed around him. Joe made her happier than she'd been in all her life. He made her feel more alive—and more angry—than she had ever thought possible. And she'd behaved foolishly—throwing insults down the elevator shaft!

Before their marriage, fighting Joe—fair or foul—hadn't been a problem. But since their wedding day he'd run in the opposite direction every time they had exchanged words.

Sable felt a small, sad smile touch the corners of her mouth. Poor Joe! He wasn't the only one running away.

It was time for both of them to face a few homegrown truths....

JOE MARCHED to the back of the building and began climbing the ladder to the first roof.

"Hey, boss! Where's your lovely lady?" one of the crewmen called out.

"She's on her way home. So you can quit ogling and start working again."

He stepped gingerly over the red-tiled roof to check the flashing around the pipes. But his mind was elsewhere. He could still see the wariness in her eyes when she'd asked if he needed more money. More of *her* money! That hurt. What was she thinking of, asking that? Did Sable honestly believe he was after her money?

He had tried so hard to show her how much he cared, but it seemed that everything he did backfired on him. Was asking her to love him, the way a woman loves a man, too much?

What he wanted made him face his feelings for Sable. The plain, stark truth was that he loved her. She couldn't have hurt him this much if he didn't.

He wanted to be her lover.

He craved to be her hero.

He just didn't know how.

The only thing he knew how to be was a lover. He'd had no practice at anything else. Being a lover was easy. You sweet-talked the woman, took her to bed and showed her your emotions in action.

But Sable needed more than that. He just didn't know what. Hell, for fear of making a bad situation worse, he'd even gone out of his way not to argue with her! But instead of being happy about it, it seemed to have made her even angrier.

"There's just no pleasing her," he muttered.

That wasn't true, but he wasn't sure anymore what the truth looked like. He was confused. And the only other person he could blame beside himself was Sable.

He'd stay out of her way until he came up with another plan of action. Sooner or later he *would* win over the fair Sable to his way of thinking. They were going to have a real marriage, and he was going to win her trust....

SABLE PACED THE KITCHEN, waiting for Joe to return home. By nine o'clock, she knew it was going to be another of his "late" nights. Emotionally drained, she sat down at the kitchen table and dropped her head into her hands.

Talia strolled in, placed her manicure set on the table and slouched into a chair across from her sister. "What's the matter?"

"Nothing."

"Sure," Talia drawled, creaming her cuticles.

"Joe didn't come home for dinner," Sable said disconsolately.

"I noticed he wasn't in his usual seat. Maybe he's still pushing for the original date for the track opening."

Sable glanced up. "You know about that?"

"Sure. Don't you?" Talia looked as surprised as Sable felt.

"Yes. But how did you find out?"

"Joe told me."

"When?"

Talia shrugged. "A week or two ago."

Sable's expression told her to continue.

"I couldn't sleep, so I came in here and made some cocoa. Then Joe came in and we talked about the track. He said he was fighting the deadlines and that he thought he could make the racing commission's contract, but it would take hard work."

"I see."

But Sable didn't see. How could he talk to Talia so easily and not speak to her at all? She was his *wife*, for heaven's sake! He should be able to talk to her about everything!

That wasn't true.

To keep him from finding out how vulnerable she was, she had purposely put up barriers he couldn't penetrate. She'd kept things from him, telling herself that he wouldn't understand. But she'd thought he wanted it that way, too. Could she have been wrong? And if so, how many other things was she wrong about? She was afraid to guess.

"Sable?" Talia's voice pierced her thoughts. "Did you and Joe make up today?"

"No," she admitted. "We started out fine, but ended up in a shouting match. Or rather, I yelled. He just walked away, as usual."

"Really? What's he trying to do, steal your act?"

"I don't walk away."

"No? So you've discussed the fact that our father was a drunk? And that's why there's no liquor in the house?"

"That's our business. Our *old* business. No one else needs to know that," Sable declared stiffly.

"I see," Talia mused. "And have you mentioned the LaCroix letter to him?"

"I mentioned it," Sable said, aware that she was hedging.

"And what did he say?"

"Not much," Sable muttered reluctantly.

"Boy! For a man who likes to talk as much as he does, he sure acts strange around you." Talia gave her an innocent look. "I wonder why?"

"I don't know."

"And he talks to Jonathan all the time, too," Talia added, her gaze still glued to her sister.

"I know," Sable said morosely. She didn't need to hear about the difference between Joe's attitude toward her and toward others.

"Yet the one woman he wants to talk about, he doesn't seem to talk to."

Sable stared through narrowed eyes at her sister. "What are you hinting at, Talia?"

The girl quickly began buffing her nails. "Nothing. I just think it's odd. It sounds as if the man has a bad case of love."

Sable bristled. Love? It was ridiculous. She'd had a man in love with her once. She would certainly recognize the signals. What Joe felt for her was more likely... lust. Damn!

"You're insane, Talia. That's the teenager in you. You think every problem has to do with love. In the adult world it's very different."

"Can't tell by me," Talia said breezily, holding her hand out for inspection. "I know about money problems and health problems. I know about puppy love and teenage problems. I even see great similarities. But if you say they're not the same, I guess you're right. I'm not all that familiar with adult hang-ups."

Sable's patience came to an end. "Well, the next time you think about love, think twice."

Talia stared at her for a moment, a frown etching her brow. "What would you say if I told you I was in love?"

"I'd say you're too young." Sable stood and smiled down at her younger sister. "And I'd say that, though the symptoms look the same, in your case it has to be puppy love."

"Really? What makes my feelings of love any different than yours?"

"Because I'm older."

Talia grinned. "Then you admit you love Joe."

"I didn't say that." Sable knew she was hedging again.

"Not in so many words. But you *did* admit it. Don't forget, you were only a kid when John swept you off your feet."

"And I was still too young to understand the kind of commitment it took to make a marriage work. I was just lucky that John cared enough to allow me to grow up and make my mistakes."

"So," Talia said thoughtfully. "As an adult, Joe is the only love interest you've ever had."

Sable gave up on her younger sister's logic. "Don't play word games with me, Talia. I'm too tired. In fact I'm going to bed."

"Sleep well." Talia's singsong voice grated on Sable's nerves as she walked down the hall to her room.

Sable realized that she was past being tired. She was punchy with exhaustion. Why else would she want to pull the covers over her head and hide from the world?

Instead she reached for a new romance novel and tried to concentrate on reading. But her heart wasn't in it and she finally gave up. It was another, long half hour before she slept. Every time she closed her eyes, she imagined Joe's head resting against her breasts, his arms around her waist and back. And his dark hair touching her cheek. He'd felt so wonderful. . . .

JOE WALKED in the back door in a mean mood, one he couldn't quite justify.

Talia, eyes bright with interest, was seated at the kitchen table. She watched him walk to the refrigerator and pull out a chilled beer. "And a good evening to you, too," she murmured.

"What are you doing up, squirt?" He drank down the beer and threw the can away.

Talia waved her hands at him. "My nails aren't dry yet."

Joe's gaze darted about the room. "Did Sable go to bed?"

Talia nodded. "She said she was exhausted. Even though she wanted to talk to you, she couldn't keep her eyes open."

"What does she want to talk to me about?" Joe opened the fridge door again, scanned the shelves and took out a plate of fried chicken wrapped in clear plastic.

"I don't know. Something about an apology, but I'm not sure. She wasn't in a good mood."

"She wasn't?"

Talia shook her head.

Joe smiled and put the chicken onto the table. It was nice to know he wasn't the only one who had problems understanding this complicated marriage.

"Any clues?"

"None. Sable was always pretty secretive, even as a teenager. It's her nature." Talia leaned closer and spoke in a low tone. "When she was young, she didn't have anyone to confide in, so she kept it all inside. Not like me. I had her to talk to. She'd solve all my problems and make me feel good about myself into the bargain. Too bad there weren't three of us. Then she could have had a big sister to confide in."

Talia hadn't mentioned their mother. Joe had a feeling that Sable had played that part.

"No friends at all?" he asked, a skeptical look in his eye.

"None," Talia told him him. "Our aunt never approved of anyone Sable brought home. So Sable stopped trying. Personally I think that's why she's so shy. She hides behind a bluff."

Joe took a bite from his chicken drumstick, then put it back onto the plate. His appetite had disappeared. "What made Sable jump to the conclusion that the LaCroix wanted to take Jonathan away from her?"

"The LaCroix family," Talia answered promptly. "To tell the truth, I don't know if they would have or not now. But we wouldn't take that chance. I'd say, judging by their visit, that they've finally seen the error of their ways. It's a good thing, too. We wouldn't want Jonathan to go through what we did."

Joe's gaze pinned Talia to her chair. He saw her squirm uncomfortably. "What do you mean, go through what you did?"

"Don't you know?" Talia was as surprised as Joe seemed to be. "I was just three when our parents divorced, so I only remember the later stages of the mess."

Joe still looked blank.

Her tone was somber as she slowly began the story. "Our parents fought over custody of Sable and me for more than two years. My mother accused my father of bedding every woman in Mobile and the surrounding area at least once, and some twice. My father maintained that my mother had done even worse—everything but sell state secrets."

"They sound like real nice people." Joe's voice was laced with sarcasm.

"They tore each other apart, both in and out of court."

Understanding flooded Joe. "No wonder," he murmured under his breath.

Talia's tone grew bitter. "They didn't care about us. They just wanted to get back at each other. They were willing to say or do anything to mortally wound each other."

Joe stared at the teenage girl. "What happened?"

Talia gazed at her fingers as if she were memorizing the curve of each nail. She glanced up, then back down, her face pale. "Well, the kicker to this whole thing is that two years after my mother won us in the custody suit, she died. And by that time our father had disappeared."

"You mean you never saw him after all the court battles? He never visited you two?" Joe asked, incredulous.

"No. Once the trial was over he disappeared. When the court tracked him down in Atlanta, he didn't want us. He told the judge he didn't know what to do with children he no longer knew, but the court, being just, gave us to him, anyway."

"You weren't raised by him, though, were you?"

"No." Talia shook her head, her eyes still staring down at the table. "After a few disastrous weeks with him and his new wife and son, we were given to his maiden aunt in Mobile. She took us—and a healthy check—once a month."

The breath whooshed from Joe's lungs. "It sounds like a childhood in hell."

For the first time he saw a sheen of tears in Talia's eyes. She shrugged. "It wasn't Aunt Diedra's fault. She just didn't know what to do with two girls. She did the best she could in the best way she knew how. She just didn't know how."

"And your dad?"

Talia closed her eyes, then blinked rapidly. "My father didn't want us to interfere with his new life. He didn't want us to see that his drinking had ruined another family. His second family."

"Do you ever see him?" Joe asked as gently as he could.

"We received a notice that he'd died, just weeks after John did. He was drunk and driving home in a rainstorm. Everything he had was left to his son." Talia glanced up, but she still couldn't look at Joe. And there was a very distinct catch in her voice that she couldn't hide. "It makes sense, I guess. Our half brother was the one who had to live with that pitiful man all those years. Not us. We got Aunt Diedra instead."

"Sounds as though neither was a bargain," Joe observed, realizing now why Sable was so fearful of drink. Talia and Sable had probably seen things he never had, experienced pain he'd never had to live through. For the first time in his life he saw the advantages of being an orphan.

"No wonder you're so grown-up for your age."

A dimple tempered the sadness in Talia's young face. It was then that Joe realized Talia was as good at hiding the truth of her emotions as her older sister.

"Thank you, kind sir, for noticing. Remember that the next time I try for a new curfew."

"If I don't, you'll remind me," he stated dryly, hoping to wring another small smile from her.

He succeeded. "Right on."

Joe stood up, wrapped the remains of the chicken in its plastic shroud and put it back into the refrigerator. "But right now it's time for bed. Curfew or not."

"No school in the morning."

"No, but you still need your beauty sleep," he teasingly reminded her. "Unless you want to look old before your time."

"No, thanks." Talia manufactured a sigh as she gathered up her manicure set. "Someday some man is going to be grateful that I look young and vibrant."

"Anyone I know?" Joe inquired with a grin.

"Yes." She ducked her head and walked under his arm as he reached for the light switch. "But I'm not telling, so don't bother to ask."

"I won't," he whispered as they reached the bedroom wing. "I've got my own troubles."

Joe smiled at the girl. He couldn't help feeling protective toward her. She was the sister he'd never had.

Talia rose swiftly on tiptoe and brushed a quick kiss onto his cheek. Before he could react, she was down the hall, entering her bedroom. "Good night," she called softly. "And thanks for listening."

"Good night. Sleep well," he answered. Her door closed, but Joe remained in the darkened hallway. He stared across the small space that separated his room from Sable's.

So Sable had had every reason to panic at the thought of a custody suit for Jonathan. She was nine years older than Talia and had understood everything that happened. Watching your parents tear each other apart was bad enough, but knowing they didn't want you as much as they professed to had to be a horrible experience.

Now it all made sense. Sable was cool and aloof with everyone—except Jonathan and Talia. With them she was as protective as a lioness sensing danger for her cubs. The only time she'd let her guard down with him had been when the LaCroix came to visit, and he'd screwed that up royally. He'd jumped in and accused her of wanting marriage for some reason other than her son.

He'd been wrong. Dead wrong.

She had never wanted Joe personally. She had wanted exactly what she'd said up front: a marriage to guarantee she'd keep custody of her son. He was the one who had assumed she wanted more.

He'd acted like a stupid fool.

He walked across the hall and slowly turned the knob. Opening the door, he stepped inside.

"Sable?"

There was no answer. Joe walked quietly to the side of her bed and stared down at the slim form nestled there. She was curled on her side, facing the window. The sheet was pushed down to her waist, displaying creamy-vanilla skin and the sensuous fullness of her breasts. His hands itched to touch the slope of waist, hip and legs. Her scent seemed to permeate the room, reminding him of sunshine and flowers and soft, spring breezes. Memories of making love to her brought back his hunger for the sweet taste of nectar on her skin.

His legs went weak at the thought of lying beside her,

then taking her into his arms and holding on for dear life as she took him to heaven.

He had to get out of here. Right now. With her image burned on his brain, he walked out and into his own room.

Checking on Sable had been a mistake. His body told him that leaving her had been another. But he'd had no choice. It was either love or conquer. And something also told him that conquering Sable in bed would be no victory. The ultimate test would be to overcome her doubts, so that he could live happily with her. Forever.

8

PROBLEMS continued unabated at the track. The pump system for the pond broke and had to be replaced. Six of the newly planted trees died within a week. The bar refrigeration system wouldn't cool.

Joe was gone at dawn and came home after midnight. But now it was because he had no choice. Now, when he wanted to be home, he couldn't be. He missed his early morning playtime with Jonathan. He missed Talia's funny bantering.

But most of all he missed Sable.

Sometimes, working at his desk, he was able to totally concentrate on the problems of the racetrack. But Sable always hovered at the edges of his mind. And whenever he did manage to focus his attention on business, Sable invariably appeared with his lunch.

The opening was less than three weeks away, and for the past two days rain had all but stopped the workmen's progress. After a brief glimpse of sun, the sky had clouded up again. As Joe walked the grounds to check on what remained to be done, he was afraid they were in for another unproductive day. He couldn't afford the time.

But if the workmen had to wait for the weather to change, Joe had a desk piled high with paperwork. He walked into his office wet and edgy. A hot casserole dish, sitting in the middle of his desk, told him that Sable had been there. The place setting was perfect. Knife, spoon and napkin were on the right, the fork on the left. Still-warm, crusty bread and a light fruit salad were in two other containers. And today she'd given him a choice. A mug and a glass stood on either side of his plate, along with a thermos of hot coffee and one of iced tea.

Joe found himself grinning. No matter what, Sable would neither buy nor drink beer.

He lifted the heavy plastic lid and sniffed. When the savory aroma of fish stew filled his nostrils, he realized he was hungry.

Sandy, Joe's right-hand man, appeared in the doorway. "Hey, boss..." He broke off and stared at the feast. "Wow. The rest of us are eating dried-out fast food, and you're being catered. Now *that*'s what being a boss is all about."

"Quit your complaining," Joe said with a chuckle. "My wife cooked this and brought it over."

Sandy's eyes rounded. "Think she might send enough for two?" he asked hopefully.

"Not a chance," Joe told him firmly. "You've got your own wife. Let her do the cooking."

Sandy stretched out in the chair across the desk, taking off his worn baseball cap to wipe his brow. "Never mind. I think I like fast food better than her cooking."

"It can't be that bad," Joe admonished, biting into a crusty piece of bread.

"It isn't. It's just that I'm not into kiddy food. She grills peanut butter sandwiches and makes pancakes in weird animal shapes. And at night she thinks that macaroni and cheese and a salad are a complete meal."

Joe shivered. "That's disgusting."

"Yeah." Sandy looked woeful. "I manage the best I can," he added with a sigh. They both avoided looking at the slight potbelly Sandy was growing.

"Well, you'll have a good meal when we finish this project. On the last day I'm having a barbecue for the crew." Joe's eyes twinkled.

"Really? Wow, that's great!" Sandy exclaimed. "Are we allowed to bring our spouses? You know, so we can kinda brag about the jobs we done?"

Joe hadn't thought about it, but the idea did make sense. After the enormous pressure they'd been under this past month, everyone needed a break. "Why not? We'll invite the families, too." Joe grinned. Sable might enjoy it.

Sandy stood up. "I'll tell the guys. It'll give them something to look forward to."

"Fine." Joe leaned back, pleasantly full. "I'll set it up and let you know the date."

Sandy surveyed Joe's suddenly relaxed attitude. "You know, boss, marriage must agree with you. At least you don't look bone edgy anymore."

"And that's supposed to be due to marriage?" Joe inquired, raising his brows.

Sandy shrugged. "Why not? Nobody can take care of a man like a good woman."

"And what does the woman get?" Joe leaned back. He'd never really discussed marriage with anyone before. Hell, he didn't even know what it took to make a good marriage. Sandy's observations might be help-ful.

"Oh, you know women. They like to feel needed," Sandy said as he strolled toward the door. "They also like to have you around some. You'd be a lot better off if you took more time to just sit still for a while."

"I'll do that," Joe said dryly. "Right after we're finished."

"Have you ever heard of delegation? You used that word a lot when we first started. But in the past month it seems you decided to finish this place all by yourself."

"Maybe," Joe hedged. "Maybe not."

"Delegate," Sandy muttered, walking away. "I always liked the sound of that word. It sounds like big business. And success."

Joe got his point. Sandy was right. He'd been running so hard, he wasn't getting as much accomplished as when he'd had weekly staff meetings to distribute the work. Then he'd been able to concentrate on problem areas. Perhaps it was time to go back to the system that worked best.

Something else Sandy had said made a lot of sense. Women like to feel needed. It was worth a try.

He picked up the phone. When Sable answered, he decided to plunge in without giving her time to stall, or worse, hang up on him.

"Sable, can you do me a favor and find a good catering company for a barbecue? We'll need a beer company for at least six kegs. Maybe some wine for the women and soft drinks for the kids."

"When and where? How many people?" Her tone was all business.

"It's for the contracting crew when they finish this project. It will be two weeks from Friday, and there should be . . ." He totaled the number of people on his payroll and tripled it. "Three hundred people. One hundred crewmen, and the rest are wives and children." He took a deep breath.

"You're really asking me to arrange this?" Her voice seemed to dance down his spine. He could get addicted to its lilting tone.

"If you can." He swallowed hard. It wasn't easy to talk to her and not react.

"Of course I can. I'll start the arrangements, then go over them with you."

She sounded so happy. Suddenly he wished he was home with her. He should be grateful for small favors. At least she was talking to him. Maybe he'd call her more often. They seemed to get along much better this way.

"Joe?"

"I'm here." He tried to focus on her words, not the sensuous notes that were turning his body to fire.

"Can you give me more information?"

"I will as soon as I have some," he promised. "By the way, lunch was delicious. Thank you."

"You're welcome," she said softly, then hung up.

For the rest of the problem-filled day Joe Lombardi had a smile on his face.

BY THAT EVENING Sable had figures from two local catering companies, as well as the cost of beer kegs. She had put together several possible menus for the barbecue. She also had a lot of questions.

Excited though she was, disappointment took over when Joe didn't come home for dinner. Again nine o'clock rolled around with no Joe. At midnight she curled up in bed and reached for a romance novel. She tried to pretend everything was okay, but felt so low that she could have easily crawled through the house on her stomach.

For a little while this afternoon Sable had believed the cold war was over. She'd thought that she and Joe might start talking to each other again. Maybe that would help restore their faltering marriage. Then Joe might think about entering her bed once more.

The hero in her book didn't hesitate to talk. He told the heroine everything—especially how much he loved her.

But how many heroes were bought? she wondered. *Stop it!* she told her wayward thoughts. It wasn't fair. She'd asked him to take the money, and now she resented that fact.

It didn't make sense.

As she drifted off to sleep, the hero in her fantasies looked just like Joe.

She woke to hear water splashing against tile. The clock told her it was past five in the morning.

Slipping on her robe, Sable followed the sound across the hall, through Joe's open door and into his wide-open bathroom. Steam fogged the mirrors and hung in the air. The see-through shower curtain was also misted, but she could see Joe's silhouette, his bent head directly under the shower. Water streamed off his broad shoulders and back.

Her pulse beat quickened at the sight. Sable cleared her throat. "Joe? Are you all right?"

His head snapped up. "As right as I'll ever be," he muttered, spewing water from his mouth. "What are you doing up at this hour?"

"I could ask you the same thing."

"I just got home," he said tiredly. "The air conditioning system wouldn't filter properly, and we spent all night working on it."

"You need some sleep!" she exclaimed. Then she realized that he already knew that and blushed at the absurdity of her remark.

"I need to sleep with you. But I guess that isn't possible." He turned the water off. "So I suggest you get your sweet little body out of here, while I grab an hour's shut-eye before my next meeting."

Sable stood quite still. His words had touched her own sleep-fogged emotions, harmonizing with needs she'd pretended didn't exist. As she watched him reach for the navy bath sheet hanging on the rack behind him to dry his hair, her needs burst into flame.

He dried off quickly with precise movements, wrapped the towel snugly around his waist and pulled the curtain aside. "Looking for something?" His tone was dry, even gruff. His eyes scanned her body impersonally.

"A bed partner."

He stared at her a moment, then slowly shook his head. "Oh, no, you don't. The last time you issued that invitation, I got chewed out for being in the wrong place at the wrong time. Never again."

Guilt flooded her, but didn't suppress the desire to be touched. "I'm sorry," she whispered.

"So am I." He eased past her to the counter and brushed his thick, wet hair into order. When it held a semblance of style, he dropped the brush and headed toward the bed. "Good night, Sable. Close the door on your way out."

He set his alarm and put it back onto the nightstand. With a brief tug, the towel dropped to the floor and Joe slipped into bed, his strong, tanned body covered by the sheet.

Sable still didn't move. Even after Joe flipped off the light above his head, she stood there, staring into the darkness, torn between running to Joe and running away.

"Good night, Sable." His voice was firm.

"Good night," she answered.

Then she closed the bedroom door and joined him. Pulling aside the sheet, she slipped into bed, next to him. Suddenly she stopped, at a loss. What came next? She hadn't planned that far ahead. In fact she hadn't planned at all.

She lay stiffly beside him, afraid to move, embarrassed to be there. Why hadn't she thought this through before making a complete fool of herself?

"Are you comfortable?" Joe growled, his voice menacing in the dark.

"Yes," she lied.

"Well, I'm not," he complained.

Turning over, he pulled her into his strong, warm arms. Crooking one leg over her thigh and laying his head next to hers, he sighed and fell instantly into a deep sleep.

Surprisingly, so did Sable.

SABLE BARELY HEARD Joe, leaving with Johnny. She slept until almost noon, awakening only when the sun streaked across Joe's bed. Stretching, she stared at the ceiling. She quivered, remembering Joe holding her tightly against him while he slept.

Happy, she went about her tasks, remembering how bold she'd been.

After school, Sable took Jonathan and Talia into Conroe for some shopping. Talia had been wanting new clothes befitting her senior status. Luckily, the little city just twenty-five miles from Houston had some nice boutiques filled with the usual fad fare for teenagers.

Waiting for Talia to emerge from the dressing room, Sable became aware that time was passing too fast. At this time next year, her sister would be entering college. She had spent so much of her life looking after Talia that she didn't know how she would deal with it.

Talia reappeared, twirling for her little nephew.

"I just realized. You'll be starting college this time next year," Sable said quietly.

"I know." Talia's eyes lighted up with excitement. "I'm aiming for Vassar. But if I can't go there, I'll try Harvard."

A lump grew in Sable's throat. "So far away? I thought we discussed Tulane?" The university was only one state away.

"We did. But that's my third choice, not my first. And with my grades and activities I should be able to qualify for any Ivy League school. I'm already filing my preadmission applications."

"I see," Sable said slowly.

Talia slipped back into the dressing room. Sable's good mood was gone. She was losing a part of her family, and there didn't seem to be a thing she could do to change it.

"Mommy cry?" Jonathan stroked her cheek softly. His big, beautiful eyes were full of sympathy.

Sable picked him up and gave him a squeeze, loving the little-boy scent of him. "No, darling. Mommy's fine."

He rubbed his nose against hers. "Tally crying?"

"No, honey. She's fine, too."

"Good," he said, getting down to explore a shirt rack next to them. As long as everyone he cared for was fine, so was he. Sable wished her feelings were so simple.

On the way home, the subject was brought up again, this time by Talia. "Sable, you know that no matter what college I choose, I'll be living in a dorm, right?"

"Of course. I just didn't realize it would be so far away." She smiled, trying to disguise her sadness.

With Talia gone, Sable's loneliness would be even more pronounced. She didn't have any close friends, and couldn't even talk to her husband. She'd have no one to share her thoughts with.

Talia's hand briefly covered Sable's on the steering wheel. "It's one of the reasons I was so pleased to meet Joe. He's perfect for you. You could be the housewife you always wanted to be, and I wouldn't have to worry about you. You could even have more children, which is exactly what you and Jonathan need. You always said you wanted half a dozen."

"You worry about me?" she asked incredulously, zeroing in on her sister's admission.

"Do you think you're the only one who worries?" Talia asked. "Sometimes you're such a babe in the woods. I worry about people taking advantage of you. Joe wouldn't do that. That's why I like him."

"You don't know Joe," Sable protested, suddenly realizing what Talia had said about children.

"I know him better than you do," Talia declared. "Joe and I have talked lots at night. You two have so much in common."

"Yes." Sable tried to keep her voice from shaking. "We both have a nosy teenager under our roof."

"There you go again!"

"What do you mean?

"Every time I try to tell you something, you bring up my age as a barrier to common sense. It's as if you don't want me to be right!" Talia exclaimed. "Are you so darn afraid of the truth?"

"I'm not afraid of anything." Sable turned the car into the driveway. "And you constantly put your nose in where it doesn't belong. Joe and I will work out our problems because they're our problems, not because you've interfered."

Talia faced forward and crossed her arms over her chest. "Not if you're not forced to, you won't," she muttered. "You've spent a lifetime trying to make peace by keeping quiet or running away. Why change now?"

"I never run away!" Sable answered tersely, wondering where in heaven her little sister could have gotten such ideas. "And there's nothing wrong with trying to keep peace. If I hadn't done it when you were growing up, your home life would have been even worse."

"Right. Our aunt might have had to change her tune on a few things—if she'd been bucked. Instead, we did whatever she wanted, and she never knew how much she hurt both of us. Auntie could quote us to the penny exactly how much we owed her for our room and board and the trouble she went through. And you always agreed—verbally, at least. It was easier to run away than stand up to her and quote the amount of money our father gave her every month to take care of us."

Sable couldn't fight that. It was true. Sometimes she'd wanted to say what she felt, but she'd never found the nerve. "And if anyone runs away in this situation, it's Joe."

"Great. Now we have two people who run away. And you're supposed to make a home together," Talia said, plainly disgusted.

"That's it," she stated, teeth clenched in anger. "You can keep your opinions to yourself from now on. I will handle Joe. I'm his wife."

"Hooray, you noticed," Talia answered sarcastically, just seconds before jumping out of the car and stalking to the back door.

"Talia!"

Sable's call was ignored.

Frustration welled inside her, but there was little she could do at the moment except carry in the shopping bags. Once more Talia's darts had hit home, and once more Sable hadn't been agile enough to dodge them. Her life was topsy-turvy, and Sable didn't seem to have the know-how or experience to straighten it out.

TALIA DIDN'T come out of her room all evening. For that Sable was grateful. She wasn't up to handling a confrontation with a teen whose energy level in sleep was more than Sable's awake.

But late that night as she lay in bed, staring at the dark ceiling, Sable wondered how much of what Talia said was true. Sable had accused Joe of running away, but was she doing the same thing? Was she avoiding issues? Did she fear problems that might end their relationship?

The answer was a resounding yes.

Her biggest stumbling block was that, having paid for a groom, she didn't believe the affection he showed her. Anything he did could be motivated by guilt, after all.

Last night she had secretly hoped that being with Joe, showing that she cared for him, would somehow make their past arguments fade away. It was a stupid wish but it was what she'd dreamed of—an easy solution.

She fell into a troubled sleep. It wasn't until she was securely held in Joe's strong arms, his warm breath caressing her shoulder, that she slept deeply.

When she awakened again, Prince Charming was gone.

JOE CONTINUED to push himself to ensure that the racetrack would run smoothly. His investment was his lifeblood. The track had to pass the racing commission's standards. He was dead on his feet, yet afraid to go home early, for fear Sable would confront him with more problems—problems he couldn't handle. At least at work he knew there was a solution. That wasn't the case at home.

Every time he remembered the morning Sable had slipped into his bed, his body tensed. She was the sweetest, most desirable, most stubborn woman he'd ever met. And he wanted her. Completely.

It was really funny, he thought. Her money had brought them together. But right now it was keeping them apart. He had to open this track on time, so he could pay her back as quickly as possible. That would be one obstacle out of the way. Then he'd only have a million others to deal with.

Then another solution appeared. The wife of one of his workers did housework, he learned, so he hired her to help take some of the cleaning chores off Sable's back. The house, after all, was huge, even though Sable had never complained about being designated housekeeper. In fact she hadn't complained about anything he'd thrown her way—except himself.

On that subject, he remembered, she'd been extremely vocal. Even in front of Talia.

He wished an answer to his dilemma would spring forth, but his mind was a blank. It didn't work the same way a woman's did, he decided. And frustration was the price he was paying for that. But when the track was completed, he would tackle the job of understanding his recalcitrant wife.

In the meantime he'd sneak home just in time to catch a little sleep with her. It was the only thing she seemed to want or allow. And although restraint wasn't the most pleasant feeling in the world, it was better than not having her in his arms at all.

It had taken a while to face the bitter truth about himself. And the revelation hadn't come like a thunderbolt, but more like a light spring rain. He loved Sable. He loved her in all the ways a man could love a woman. He wanted to share his life with her, to have her by his side in times of triumph and trouble.

He wanted Sable to love him as much as he loved her.

"Work on the possible, Lombardi," he muttered. "Don't wish for the impossible."

He remembered that she had seemed thrilled when he gave her the party plans to work on. Maybe if he included her in more of the everyday workings of the ranch, she'd enjoy that, too. The thought brought a smile to his face.

Picking up the phone, he dialed home. When Sable's voice came over the line, his body tensed. She always affected him that way.

"I was wondering if you could do me a favor the next time you're in town," Joe asked.

"Sure. What is it?" She sounded a little breathless. He liked that. "Go by Smitty's and pick up four cases of beer for the bunkhouse. Put it on my tab."

"Four cases of beer?"

"Yes. Because we're so far out of town, I keep beer on hand for the boys. That way they can relax in the evening without leaving the property. I don't have to worry about them going on a toot."

"Isn't four cases a lot? They could get drunk."

"They're big boys," Joe replied, amused. "They can take care of themselves.

When he hung up, he was still smiling.

SABLE STARED out the kitchen window, wondering how many of those beers Joe would drink if he wasn't so tied up with the track. She had to admit that she'd never seen him drunk or disorderly. Nor had she seen the men in the bunkhouse that way. But that didn't mean they couldn't do it.

She'd go into town for beer in the morning. Meanwhile she'd figure out another way for the boys to be entertained. There had to be something else they could do besides drink beer.

That night she slipped into Joe's bed and read until midnight. When she turned out the light, she fell again into a restless sleep. Only when he climbed in beside her and rested his arm on her waist did she settle down.

As usual, he was gone by the time she awakened. But his scent lingered on the pillow next to hers. She lifted it and buried her face in the soft fabric, wishing for the real thing.

At midafternoon Sable returned from Conroe with the beer Joe had requested. She put the brew into the bunkhouse refrigerator, then hurried back to the house.

A short time later Joe entered the house by the back door and called her name. Sable walked into the kitchen, widening her eyes when she realized she was looking at a little boy in a man's body. "What's going on?"

He grinned, his eyes alight with mischief. "Come on, we're going horseback riding," he said, grabbing her hand and starting to head outside. "The air conditioning system is in and working, and I'm playing hooky."

"Let me get dressed!" she exclaimed, delighted with his happy mood. "But shouldn't you be catching up on your sleep?"

"I need a horseback ride, and no, I don't want to sleep." He stared down at her, his hand still firmly holding hers. "It's the farthest thing from my mind."

The gleam in his eye said he wanted something else entirely. "Let me put on my riding boots," she said.

Lightning swift, she ran to her room and pulled out a pair of Moroccan leather ankle boots. Her movements rivaling the fast forward action of a camera, she changed and ran back out again. Joe was standing in the kitchen, talking to Talia.

He took Sable's hand again and led her out to the barn. His plans had apparently been made before he came into the house, for their horses were saddled and ready to go. Jed held the reins, the smug smile on his face reminding her of the one she'd seen on Talia's.

Giving her a hand up, Joe let his fingers slip down her calf to give her ankle a squeeze. Sable chuckled. It felt so good to do something spontaneously, to have fun for a change.

They began with a canter, Joe leading the way behind the barn and across the field. As they neared a path that ribboned its way through the woods, they trotted. The warm afternoon breeze filtered through Sable's hair and blouse as if proclaiming her freedom.

Her bubbling laughter danced in the air.

Recklessness had never been a part of her makeup, but suddenly she was filled with it. At the end of the trail through the woods, Sable glanced over her shoulder. With a triumphant smile and a light kick to her horse, she urged him into a gallop and sailed past Joe.

His surprise was her advantage. Within a minute or two she was far ahead, aiming for the sloping riverbank. But by the time she pulled the reins to slow down, the gap had closed considerably. Still, when she reached the water's edge and the shelter of a huge willow tree, she waited impatiently for Joe to join her.

A tense excitement stirred the air as he halted his own horse and swung to the ground to stand by her side. In a single swift movement he was lifting her down and into his arms.

His blue eyes no longer danced with mischief. Instead the intensity of his gaze seared her.

"I've finally got you to myself. No prying eyes anywhere in sight. No Johnny, no Talia, no ranch hands."

"No one."

"You're beautiful."

Her fingers traced one dark brow. "If you say so."

There was no doubt as to what he wanted. Every muscle in his body was tense.

Sable reveled in the reckless abandon she saw in his eyes. Taking Joe's face between her hands, she placed her parted lips on his. Her tongue flicked against his moist warmth, and a moan echoed between them like a hollow cry for help.

His arms clasped her waist, pinning her body against his hardness. But it wasn't enough.

He was hungry. He was a starving man.

Strong, impatient hands unzipped her jeans and loosened them enough to cup the ripe softness of her derriere in his palms, cradling her against the jutting hardness of his own need.

Sable stared up at him. His jaw was tight, his breathing shallow.

"Are you going to deny me?" His voice was a mere rasp.

Her hand trailed lightly over his jaw. "No," she whispered. "Denying ourselves would be silly at this point, don't you think?"

Her hands drifted lightly from his shoulders to his chest, and she slowly undid his shirt, exposing the dark hair. Occasionally her hand passed over the curls, watching them spring against her palm.

"Sable," he warned.

Her hand slipped to his zipper. She looked up, her eyes heated with the same fire that inflamed his. "Be patient."

His eyes roamed downward, and her pulse quickened in response. "I don't have any patience left. I need you. Now."

"Not yet." Standing on tiptoe, she pressed soft kisses onto his neck and chest. The fabric shifted off his shoulders and dropped to his wrists. His hands clenched tighter at her waist, pulling her even closer.

Her tongue darted out to flick one small, male nipple. His response was immediate. He took her hand and led her to him, his palm covering hers. Her eyes drooped as she leaned back her head, allowing him full view of her slender throat and the teasing, beginning fullness of her breasts.

"That's it," he muttered. With jerking movements, Joe stripped off his shirt and threw it to the ground beneath the dancing leaves of the trees. In one smooth motion he lowered her to the ground, his body covering hers, crushing her breasts against his chest. It felt so right.

His hands were everywhere, unzipping, unbuttoning, making fabric barriers between them disappear. His mouth pressed teasing kisses against the softness of her skin, until she felt as if her whole body glowed with the intense heat of his touch.

His hands were everywhere. One hand slipped to caress her belly, his fingers teasing, touching, stroking. She drew a ragged breath as anticipation seared through her. When he touched the apex of her thighs, she gasped.

When his mouth captured the peak of one full breast, she felt scalded with pleasure. "Joe, please," she whispered.

He chuckled. "Not yet," he answered, mimicking her. And then he began the most exquisite torture of all.

Sable squirmed with need, and Joe finally appeased her. When he slipped deep inside her, her cry of pleasure echoed through the summer air.

The excitement of having his flesh on hers, in her, his scent surrounding them, drew her quickly to the edge. Joe tried to be gentle. His hands shook as he lifted his torso to kiss her parted lips, the sweet line of a shoulder. But gentleness was not what she needed just then. She wanted his powerful presence to fill her until she couldn't see anything but him.

He understood that and took her to a plane she hadn't known existed. Sable clung to him as they climbed peak after peak, then spiraled back to earth in each other's arms.

His warm breath caressed her ear, his heart still pounded against hers. For a few, very special, moments they had become one perfect being. As the feeling of completeness dwindled away, Sable wanted to reach out and hold it.

But she couldn't.

Flinging his hand against his eyes, Joe rolled onto his back. The fingers of his other hand were wound in her hair, still connecting them. The sun was suddenly cold against her flesh.

Just then, one of the horses neighed to gain their attention, then nudged Joe's booted foot. They both smiled.

"That was quite a ride, lady," he muttered, his voice still a low growl.

Sable relaxed, rubbing her hand against his chest as if to reassure herself that he was still there. "Are you talking to me or the horse?" she teased.

Joe turned to face her, his eyes the darkest, most penetrating blue she'd ever seen. "I'm talking to the horse. There are no words that would begin to explain what you and I just experienced."

"Try," she coaxed.

His gaze seared her with the message that couldn't seem to come forth in words. Finally he sighed and placed a light kiss on her swollen lips. "I can't. I know you need to hear the words, and I want to say what I feel. But I can't."

"Why?"

His finger took the place of his lips as he outlined first her lips, then her chin, watching as his own darker skin touched hers. "Because I'm not sure I have the words." He sighed. "Someday, darling," he promised.

Sable swallowed her disappointment. *She* couldn't find the words to tell him she loved him. So who was she to talk?

Promising herself that soon she'd find the courage to say what was in her heart, she stood up and began to dress.

Joe leaned back and watched every move she made, his naked body gleaming in the dappled sunlight. But the possessive look in his eyes told her what he wanted to know.

It was enough to warm her heart. Someday would be soon.

9

THEIR RIDE back to the house was a slower, sweeter trip, less fraught with tension than when they had ridden out. Occasionally Joe took her hand and squeezed it lightly. Every time he did, happiness filled her, healing the pain of their earlier dissension.

From the moment she first saw him, she'd been drawn to him. And this afternoon, under the graceful willow branches that shielded them from the open, pale blue sky, with a carpet of pine needles for a bed, had been the answer to her prayers. She loved him. Her whole life revolved around him. She wanted it to stay that way. But until he committed himself to her, she'd never be happy.

She cursed the thoughts that had crept in during the dark of night, whispering that her money was the only reason he remained with her. She hated the thoughts that had suggested he was only using her. Their love-making was so much more than lust.

Once or twice Joe reined in their horses, then pulled her toward him for a kiss. Fleeting though it was, her heart beat quickly with each one. His touch was gentle, sweet, and he was reluctant to let go. He cared. He had to care or he wouldn't be this charming, this considerate after making love.

It was as if she'd been looking at everything through dark glasses, plodding through life, afraid to look for what might be out there. Then Joe had come along and made her take them off. Now the world was brighter, sweeter, sillier. And for the first time she was in love— as an adult and with an adult. This wasn't hero worship or the search for a father figure.

Everything would be wonderful from now on, she told herself. They could work out whatever little problems came their way. The tension that she'd lived with these past weeks was gone. Making love and being able to smile again made all the difference in the world. Weather forecast, she thought, sunny and mild for the rest of their lives.

Reaching the open area around the house, they sent their horses into a gallop and rode through the wide doorway to the barn together. Laughter filled the air and smiles lighted their eyes.

Totty, the hand in charge of the grounds and barns, stood leaning on a pitchfork, his face a wrinkled road map of frowns. He watched them closely, but not a muscle in his face moved.

Joe swung out of his saddle, then helped Sable dismount, treating her as if she were the most precious thing on earth. He kissed the tip of her nose. Then, pretending to whisper something into her ear, he kissed her there, too. Her cheeks glowed in response as she stood in the protective shelter of his arms.

With his arm firmly around Sable's waist, he turned toward Totty. "What's the matter, Totty? Somebody kill your best friend?"

Totty shot a wad of chaw through the doorway before speaking. "Might well have," he muttered. "Whoever you got to deliver the beer pulled a fast one on you."

Sable felt her smile slip. Not now, she thought. Not now!

"What do you mean?" Joe's arm still circled her waist, but his attention was focused on his oldest hired hand. "It was delivered, wasn't it?" His gaze flashed to Sable, then back to Totty.

"Oh, it was delivered, awright," Totty drawled. "But it ain't beer. It's some kinda soft drink that's supposed to taste like beer."

Joe's arm dropped from Sable's waist, leaving her chilled. "Is that a fact?"

Totty pushed back his battered hat and wiped his forehead with his shirt sleeve. "That's a fact," he confirmed disgustedly.

Why had she been such a fool? Why couldn't Totty have brought this up later—much later?

Unwilling to see the gathering storm in Joe's eyes, Sable grabbed the bridle, walked her horse to his stall and began to unsaddle him.

She'd felt Totty's eyes watching her walk away and realized that he had no idea who had bought the beer. It didn't give her much relief. Soon he'd know. Then she'd have one more man who wondered if there was any substance to the spoiled little socialite.

She couldn't help but hear the conversation between the two men. Her stomach roiled with each word.

"Show me what you're talking about." Joe's voice was empty of the concern and love he'd shown her just moments ago.

"Be glad ta," Totty answered. The sound of their footsteps told her they were leaving the barn and heading toward the bunkhouse—and her purchase of four cases of nonalcoholic beer.

The air whooshed from her lungs. With shaking hands Sable brushed down her horse. She didn't know what to do except to keep busy and hope that Joe wouldn't be too upset with her. Even though she often faced problems head-on, she hated confrontation, so she understood Joe's willingness to avoid an argument.

In her teen years Sable had done quite a bit of that. But when she'd married John and found he did the same thing, she'd been the one to confront trouble and find a solution. She didn't want to be in that spot again. Being a mother to a three-year-old was enough. She shouldn't have to be a mother to a grown man, too.

Besides, with Joe it was different. She was afraid of losing what little they had together if she confronted anything, and at the same time it seemed as if she did things that were intended to annoy him.

As minutes ticked by like hours, Sable felt her hackles rise. So what if she hadn't gotten the beer Joe had expected? People shouldn't be drinking. She had other things to do besides run around the countryside, buying beer for a bunch of men.

Joe's firm, booted tread announced his imminent arrival and she tensed. By the time he appeared at the stall door, she was holding her breath.

"What in the hell made you do such a stupid thing?"

His tone demanded an answer, but at that moment she couldn't think of one. His hard, angry gaze twisted her thoughts into hundreds of small knots that wouldn't unravel enough for her to form a reply.

"No one should promote drinking," she finally answered.

"Just how vindictive can you get?" His words sliced through her like a hot knife. "You take away their beer and give them six different *games* to play with?"

That was unfair! "Vindictive?" She raised her voice defensively. "I wasn't being vindictive. I was *trying* to give the men an alternative to drinking themselves into a stupor!"

"They *don't* drink themselves into a stupor!"

Her hands went to her hips, so she wouldn't be tempted to slap him. "How would you know? You're never with them! You're always worked late."

Eyes blazing with anger, Joe threw down his hat. "You're really something, you know that? You've done everything you could to show me that you hate being here. You hate my life-style. You hate me. But I've been too stupid to realize it! I've been hoping that if I was nice and a gentleman, you'd finally see some of my redeeming features, and maybe we could make a go of this farce of a marriage."

He took a step closer. Feeling menaced, Sable backed up.

"But I was dead wrong," he continued. "You'll never change. You'll always be a snob. Women can sit around all day, sipping wine and doing nothing. But a man who's worked all day in the hot sun isn't supposed to enjoy a beer as he sits on the porch at night and watches a ball game. And it's all because you decided to set yourself up as judge and jury for people you don't know and haven't cared to find out about. That's hypocritical, Sable, but I don't know why I expected anything else from you."

Joe bent to pick up his hat; it was all Sable could do not to kick him in the rear.

Anger made her shake with reaction. "That's not true!" she cried. "I've washed and ironed shirts that you could have just as easily sent to a laundry. I've cooked meals you've never eaten, and kept 'your' house as clean and neat as a pin. I've given you everything, including my money, but nothing seems to get through to you. I've got wants and needs and desires, too! But you never noticed that, either. Because you're never home!"

Joe gave her a disgusted look and began to walk out.

But Sable wasn't through with him yet. "Just because I don't earn a salary doesn't mean that I don't work as hard as you and your crew! Twice as hard!" she shouted at his retreating, grass-stained shirt.

Tears filled her eyes. Damn him! Who did he think he was to yell at her like that? Just because she bought a beer substitute instead of the real thing didn't mean that Joe could call her down.

But he hadn't, a little voice said. He'd waited to see the evidence for himself before confronting her—in private.

Oh, shut up, she told her conscience as she stomped out of the stall and headed toward the house. It wasn't worth the effort to fight back. Not when she was wrong....

JOE DIDN'T COME HOME. He left Sable a note, saying he had to go to Austin for a license review, but Sable wasn't sure if that was true.

After a week Joe returned, but seemed to be sleeping at the track. Sable apologized to Totty, who, embarrassed, brushed it off as a lack of knowledge about beer in general. At least he remained her friend, she thought. It was better than Joe's response.

Occasionally in the early evening, when she was cleaning out one of the horses' stalls, Jonathan would run next door and play on the porch with the crewmen, cheering on whatever team they were rooting for. He loved sitting with the men, and she had to admit that they were gentle with him.

But her lonely times taught her three things: she loved Joe with all her heart; Talia and Jonathan missed Joe almost as much as she did; and she wanted to make her marriage work.

When Joe made no effort to contact her, Sable finally remembered the barbecue. She still had the figures and estimates for the party, but he'd never answered her questions. Now was as good a time as any to call and get them. And if she and Joe could carry on a normal conversation for a while, all the better. Somehow she had to give herself a chance to close the gap between them.

But when she called, he wasn't there. Every hour, on the hour, she tried calling his office again. Still no answer.

By the time Talia came home, Sable was pacing the floor. Scraps of paper containing her questions were clenched in her hand.

"Will you watch Jonathan for me?" Sable asked as soon as her sister walked in the door. "I need to go to the site and speak to Joe."

"Sure," Talia replied quickly, fearing Sable would change her mind. "And tell him I said hi and I miss him around here."

"Will do," Sable promised, picking up her purse and practically running for the back door.

The drive to the track was the longest ten minutes Sable could remember. Stepping out of the car, she stared up at the roof, fully expecting to see Joe striding across the tiles.

He wasn't there.

She was amazed at how much had been done since she'd been there last. The open lobby and general seating were finished. Soft mauves and grays and a light peach gave the area a cool, serene appearance. She took the elevator up to Joe's office and was just as pleased with the look of the private club space. Similar-colored tables and chairs were comfortably arranged on every level. Wide four-story-high windows afforded a complete view of the track and gardens.

Her heels no longer echoed on concrete, but glided on pale gray, short-sheared carpet.

She heard Joe's voice as she reached the office door. Sable stopped in her tracks. Her heart pounded heavily in her breast. Her breath caught in her throat.

Then suddenly he was standing before her, a file in his hand. His eyes widened as he saw his wife. "Is something wrong?"

Even though her heart was in her throat, Sable pasted a smile onto her face. "Everything's fine. I just need some information. I thought I'd run over, since you haven't been answering your phone today."

Joe's brows lifted. "I wasn't in."

Sable laughed huskily. "I gathered. But I thought the answering machine would be on."

"It should have been. But my secretary is sick today and I probably forgot to set it."

Turning, Joe walked back to his desk and sat. Sable followed him, leaning against the corner of the desk. His face held no smile for her. There was no warmth, no eagerness to talk.

"What's your question?" he asked in a voice laced with tiredness.

Sable's heart went out to him. His face was drawn, his eyes heavy with lack of sleep. He'd obviously been working too hard. And if the blanket thrown on the long, leather couch was any indication, this really was where he slept.

"You're exhausted."

Joe ran a hand through his disheveled hair. "So what's new?" he muttered, glancing at the myriad stacks of paperwork on his desk. "Just ask me the questions, Sable. I don't need one of our usual discussions. I don't think I could survive it right now."

Sable straightened, mentally withdrawing her emotions. Obviously he didn't want to mend fences or take care of his wife and her petty problems right now. She couldn't stand it. Just the thought of living without Joe made panic well up inside until she was blinded by fear. But that panic also goaded her on.

"I was just wondering what happens next," she told him. "You've been sleeping here, traveling when you want. You haven't even pretended to be the model father our contract stipulated you would be."

She prayed he'd sweep her into his arms and tell her he loved her. But she knew better. His expression told her that much.

"What is you want, Sable?" he asked quietly. "A divorce?"

His question was like an icy slap in the face. She should have expected it, yet she hadn't. Startled, she gazed up at him. He stared back, his expression unreadable. Another stab of pain seared through her.

She swallowed. "Is that what you want?"

"Don't answer a question with a question, especially the same one I asked you," he said softly, a tiny, sad smile edging his lips. "You always were evasive about things that mean a lot to you."

She shook her head. She couldn't find her voice. "I want..." she finally managed to stammer, but couldn't complete the sentence. The words she needed just weren't there.

Joe's sigh filled the office, saying more than all the words he could have shouted. "Look, do the barbecue for me and help me get this racetrack opened. After that you can have your divorce. I just need to get this going, so I'll be able to pay back the money you . . . so graciously lent me."

The mention of the money made her flinch. But it wasn't their only problem. She thought of all the things she'd done wrong since they'd married. Guilt weighed heavily upon her, and she had promised herself she would apologize to Joe.

"I'm sorry." Her thoughts had slipped out. "For everything."

He reached out and touched her chin, his thumb outlining the clean, sweet form of it. "So am I, Sable. So am I."

"I'll do your party."

He stood up. "I know."

"And I'll do a good job."

He smiled. "I know."

"And then we'll see."

"Okay."

His hand dropped and a chill brushed her very soul. "Are you coming home tonight?" she asked, stalling for time.

"I don't know yet, Sable. I can't push myself too far. The consequences could make us both sorry."

She nodded. "Okay."

He leaned over as if a strong rope were pulling him. His lips brushed hers. "Thank you."

This time Sable walked out.

Joe watched her go, and his heart felt as if it were being ripped from his chest. He watched as she stood in front of the elevator and waited for its doors to open. By the time she disappeared, the pain was so great that all he could do was walk across the office and slump dejectedly into his desk chair.

She wanted a divorce. The thought echoed in his mind. *She wanted a divorce.* He'd hoped that she would deny it. Instead she'd agreed.

He loved her.

He loved her family.

He needed to feel a part of them. He loved feeling a part of them.

With Sable he felt complete.

How the hell could he tell her he loved her, when the money was between them, forming a wall bigger than the one in China?

Tears filmed his eyes, and he prayed that one of his men wouldn't barge in with some petty demand and find him like this. It would be hard to explain that he wasn't crying, but just feeling sorry for himself.

That inner voice spoke: *You're crying.*

The inner voice was right.

THE BARBECUE was a huge success. Joe made a short speech, thanking all his employees for their devotion to work and their spouses for their patience. The track would open in a week. The office and working crews would begin their training on Monday. Everyone applauded enthusiastically.

Sable's sharp eyes skimmed the tables laden with cooked beef, pork, chicken and sausage. Next to the hot meats were the crisp, cold salads: potato, coleslaw, cold pasta tossed with vegetables, and piles of lettuce, tomatoes and sliced, sweet onions, as well as pickles, olives and relishes.

A five-piece Western band played in the shade of the inner, general gallery. Couples danced, while others stood in groups, talking and watching the children at play.

Joe came up to stand beside Sable and casually draped an arm around her shoulders. She was sure it was simply for effect in front of the workers and their families. But, even though it was a pretense, it felt wonderful.

"Any problems?" Joe asked.

"Not yet," she said cautiously. "The catering firm seems to be doing well."

"So did you. Everything's been arranged perfectly," Joe told her quietly. "Thank you."

"You're welcome."

She didn't discount the amount of work she'd put into this party. And Joe had noticed. That made her feel even better.

A few companionable moments of silence passed before Joe spoke again. "Do you dance?"

Startled, her eyes darted to his. "A little," she admitted. "But I'm not very good.

His smile was beautiful. And heartrendingly sexy. "Don't tell me you never attended dances when you were growing up."

She couldn't stop looking at him. "I never did. I wasn't asked."

"Young boys from Mobile must be stupid," he said, slipping his arm down to clasp her hand.

"Why?"

He led her around the tables to the general gallery. "Because, even if you were only half as beautiful as you are now, they didn't have the nerve to ask. You would probably have danced if you'd been asked."

"How did you know?"

Joe chuckled, a rueful smile etching his mouth. "Because certain boys from Houston weren't too bright at that age, either."

"Neither was I," Sable admitted. "Or I would have asked them. But if you ever quote me to Talia, I'll deny every word."

He stopped in the center of the floor and turned her toward him. "Why?"

"Because she's assertive enough already. I don't think she needs any encouragement."

Joe glanced over her shoulder, then turned her around so she could she what he'd just glimpsed. "I think I agree with you." He laughed. "If I'm not mistaken, she asked Mike to dance. He never volunteers."

Sable saw the uncomfortable expression on the man's face. But she saw something else, too. No matter how much he claimed to prefer sitting on the sidelines, Mike was enchanted by Talia. And Talia glowed with an inner excitement.

Sable frowned, but Joe turned her into his arms, as one slow song blended into another, and she forgot about Talia.

Both his arms rested on her hips, his hands clasped together at the small of her back. She had no choice but to hold on to his broad shoulders. Every time he moved, she felt the tight flex of muscles beneath her palm, and it reminded Sable of other things she shouldn't be remembering at all.

Making love in the cab of a truck. Undressing in the bright, hot, summer sun and feeling the heat flow through every vein in her body, making her one with the earth and with Joe.

Her hands trailed slowly down his shoulders, stopping at the rock-hard muscles of his arms. She wanted to hold him, hug him, lay her head on his chest and tell him that she wanted him back. To hell with the divorce. To hell with everything except the two of them.

"A penny for your thoughts," he said softly.

She opened her eyes and stared up at him. He looked as though his thoughts were as serious as hers. Sable cleared her throat. "They're worth a quarter now. Inflation, you know."

"You can reach in my front pocket and get it."

The thought was enough to make her palms sweat. "I'll trust you," she finally said, her voice barely a husky whisper.

"A shame," he admonished softly. "Cowboys shouldn't be trusted. We act shy, but we know what we want and go after it."

At those encouraging words she screwed up her courage and asked, "And what do *you* want?"

Brilliant blue flashed in his eyes as he focused on her lips. Then, with an almost intimidating slowness, his glance dropped to the low V of her cream silk blouse, tucked snugly into designer jeans. His hands tightened. Then he forcibly relaxed. "No matter what it is, I don't think there's a fairy godmother with enough magic dust to give it to me."

Sable prayed he'd catch on soon. She wanted him to drag her to his office and tell her that he loved her as much as she loved him. Because of her money she couldn't say those words first. "If you don't ask, you'll never know."

His eyes narrowed. "If I did ask, I'm not sure I'm ready to hear the answer."

"Tsk, tsk, tsk," Sable murmured unsteadily. "So fainthearted for a cowboy who knows what he wants."

Their steps slowed to a stop. Still he continued to stare at her. "Sable—" Joe began.

"Hey, boss!" Joe's secretary called from the open elevator doors. "The racing commission is on the phone. They need to talk to you! Pronto!"

Joe cursed, then reluctantly pulled away. "Hold that thought," he said to her, then slipped into the elevator with Judy.

The doors closed and he was gone again.

Sable walked off the dance floor and went outside to check the tables. Her racing pulse slowly thudded down to a more normal beat. By the time Joe returned, he'd probably be all business again. He'd never remember how she'd tried to say everything but the words that would commit her to him for life. *I love you* had to be the most powerful aphrodisiac in the world—if those were the words one wanted to hear.

But if Joe didn't hear them, she'd never know if they could erase the mistakes of the past and turn their lives toward a rosy future.

And if he did? He might very well laugh in her face and tell her, "Tough luck, sweetie. . . ."

She didn't know which thought was more frightening. But she knew she had to find out.

Tonight, she promised herself. She'd tell him tonight. All he could do was make her miserable enough to run back to Louisiana like a whipped puppy, with her tail between her legs.

An hour later Joe found her talking to one of the caterers. Pulling her away, he spoke quickly, but quietly. "I have to be in a meeting with the racing commission in Austin right away. It seems that one of the senators who has to sign the licenses has had a heart attack. We have to work through the final paperwork without him, or we'll never get it done before opening. Mike's going with me."

"Don't go. Not now," she pleaded.

"I'll be back by the middle of the week." He pulled her into his arms. "So do me a favor, will you? Miss me."

It was an order, not a request. But Sable didn't care. And when his lips claimed hers for a quick, hard kiss, she still didn't mind. Her fingers curled into the fabric of his shirt, unwilling to let him go, unwilling to hold him against his will. His hands tightened at her waist, pulling her into the hardness of his body.

The next moment he was striding toward Mike, who was standing by the gate, Talia at his side. Once Joe reached him, both men kept going.

Neither one looked back.

10

REGRET was a heavy burden. Joe had sounded distracted and businesslike when he called Saturday night to give her his room number at the hotel. And Sable, temporarily open and loving, had closed up like a clam. She told herself he would call again when things eased up. But the days passed and disappointment grew as she waited for a phone call that never came.

WHEN A WOMAN knocked on the door Monday morning and announced that Joe had hired her to houseclean, Sable felt herself turn white. Apparently Joe was already replacing her.

On Tuesday there was still no word from Joe, and Sable was an emotional wreck. When John had died, she'd been devastated. She had clung to Talia and Johnny, not allowing herself to care for anyone else. She'd lost so many people in her life that she wanted to protect herself.

She had also done the same thing with Joe. When he had gotten too close to her, she'd effectively sabotaged their relationship. She'd secretly been afraid of losing him, if she acknowledged her love aloud.

Now that she had an idea of where the problem came from, she was *damned* if she would let it ruin her life. Ignoring their problems was no way to overcome them.

Her resolve once more firmly in place, she picked up the phone and dialed the number Joe had left her.

Joe's voice barked into the phone. "Hello."

"Hi," she answered brightly, her heart thumping so hard, she wondered if the whole world heard it.

"Sable? Is that you?" he asked, the curtness fading from his tone. "Is something wrong?"

"No." She laughed nervously. "I just wondered when you were returning home. I haven't heard from you lately."

"If that's a stab at my communication skills, it'll have to be one more sin to add to the already long list," he stated flatly.

Damn! She hadn't meant to sound churlish. "That wasn't what I meant at all. I was just . . . concerned that everything was going well."

"Everything's going okay, Sable." His voice was softer now, less defensive and more tired. "There's just so many necessary permits—all on different levels of government. And we need them now, even though half the people are out of town. But if everything goes well, we should be home in a day or so. And this Saturday the track can open."

"I'm glad," she said, and meant it. "You've worked so hard to see your dream come true. You deserve it."

He laughed, but it was a brittle sound. "I've worked hard for a lot of things, Sable, but they haven't materialized yet, either."

"How do you know? You aren't home to find out," she told him softly. Her heart did flip-flops as she waited for his answer.

"Oh, I know," he replied, bitterness coloring his voice.

She heard a gruff voice yell his name, and Joe covered up the mouthpiece for a minute. When he returned, he was all business again. "We'll have a long talk when I return, Sable. Goodbye."

Pushing down the receiver button, she held the phone to her breast like a talisman. Nothing had changed—except that now she knew when he was coming home—soon.

LATE IN THE NIGHT, Joe stood naked in the dark room and stared out at downtown Austin. Here he was, in the middle of one of the hottest night spots in Texas, and he couldn't care less. Before Sable came along, he would have been a part of the revelry, whooping it up with the rest of the tourists, instead of sitting in a dark hotel room, mooning over a wife who'd rather be a divorcée.

After the day's meetings, Joe had fallen into bed; weariness had dogged him this entire trip. But sleep hadn't come—it was as elusive as the night shadows beyond his window.

The full moon that hung above the buildings glared down as if it, too, were frustrated by the events of the past and anxious about the present. Joe stared at it and tried to remember how to make a wish. Over his left shoulder? Looking at the moon, or at a rising star?

Since there was no one here to see him, he decided to take a chance.

"Let Sable and me work out our problems."

The words echoed in the quiet room. That really wasn't his wish. His wish was that she might love him—blindly, unhesitatingly, and with all her heart.

But to say those words aloud would mean that wishes wouldn't come true. He knew that from experience. As a child he'd never received anything he asked for. Why should things change now?

Sable. Her skin was as translucent as the waning moon. Her hair was the color of a rich, thick, sensuous coat of her namesake. When her eyes flashed, exhibiting her many moods, it was as though all the colors of the rainbow momentarily appeared in their depths.

He should have known he was in trouble the day he met her. In fact he *had* known. He'd just chosen to ignore all the warning signs.

A loud shout of celebration rang through the night, followed by a woman's tinkling laughter. The sound reminded him of home.

Could he have misread her again? Was he wrong to hope that she wanted to reconcile their differences as much as he did?

He wanted Sable, and suddenly he didn't care who knew it. He had to let her know how he felt.

She was the most enchanting, infuriating, unusual, wonderful and impetuous woman he'd ever known. Everything was exciting when she was around, yet nothing was more calming than when she slipped her hand into his. And her smile lighted his soul.

Determination tightened his muscles. He'd get her, if he had to hire skywriters to fly over the house morning, noon and night.

Of course, there might be a simpler way....

Joe smiled his first genuine smile of the day. He had a plan that just might work.

JOE WAS DRESSED AND READY when Mike came by the following morning to pick him up.

"You look like hell," his friend commented, helping himself to some of the leftover coffee and cold toast.

Joe watched Mike through heavy-lidded eyes. Now that the sun was up, he was as tired as a bear roused from a long hibernation. "Didn't you get room service for yourself?"

Mike shook his head. "Why should I? You keep ordering food and then don't touch it. Someone should enjoy the fruits of the hotel's labor."

Joe gave his friend a speculative glance. "Speaking of enjoying—what was going on between you and Talia at the barbecue?"

Mike took a long swallow of his coffee. "Nothing, Joe. I swear it. She's just a nice kid who seems to have taken a shine to me." Mike looked flustered as he stared out the window, his coffee now forgotten.

"She's only seventeen," Joe reminded him.

"Don't you think I know that? I've got sisters myself, Joe. I'm just trying not to hurt her feelings. That's all. She's a sweet kid."

Joe sighed, knowing firsthand how tenacious—and how vulnerable—Talia was. She was also the savviest seventeen-year-old he'd ever met. "It's not going to be easy to walk that fine line between friend and romantic idol. It might be better to hurt her now than let her girlish imagination take flight."

Mike turned to pace nervously around the room. "I've tried, but she insists that we can be friends until she'd old enough to change the situation."

Laughing ruefully, Joe stopped Mike by throwing an arm around his shoulders. "Mike, relax," he ordered.

Mike tried to do as he was told. "She's a sharp little girl, Joe."

Joe chuckled. "She takes after her older sister."

"You know, she informed me that her eighteenth birthday was next July, that her favorite flowers were irises and her favorite restaurant was Vargo's on the bayou."

Both men shook their heads. "She spins quite a web, that little spider," Joe commented. "So what are you going to do?"

"I'll send her a bouquet of irises—along with a gift certificate for two for the restaurant—and a letter, telling her to invite the best boy from her school to dine with her."

Joe's brows rose. "Very clever. And very expensive."

Mike pushed up his glasses on his nose. "With the determination this girl shows at this age, she'll be chairman of the board of some major corporation in the near future. It's an investment. I'm hoping she'll hire me for her corporate business."

Joe finally relaxed, doing what he'd told Mike to do earlier. "Good planning," he said, relieved that Mike had the ability to handle a potentially dangerous situation. No wonder Sable had nicknamed her Spike.

Joe grabbed the keys off the top of the TV and headed for the door. "Let's go to that meeting and get this trip out of the way. I need to get home to my wife and sister-in-law."

"Great. Maybe you can keep that junior Mata Hari in line."

"I doubt it, Mike," Joe replied. "But I'll give it a try."

SABLE LOST WEIGHT. "Every other woman would be thrilled to lose weight. But not me. I already have to resemble a scarecrow," she muttered, ignoring the mirror as she stepped from her morning shower and dried one slim leg.

She refused to look into the mirror. Weight loss wasn't her only problem. She knew that a tinge of blue was clearly visible beneath her eyes, showing all and sundry that she hadn't been sleeping well.

What concerned her more was that she was pregnant. This morning, gathering her courage, she'd used one of those early pregnancy kits and confirmed what she'd suspected for the past two weeks.

She was carrying Joe's baby.

She was exhilarated, happy—and frightened, because she had no idea what his reaction would be.

Would he hate her? Would he see her pregnancy as a trap?

After dressing with care and determination, she brushed back her hair into a sleek roll, then studied herself in the mirror. Despite the problems, she wouldn't give this child up for all the world. This would be a baby to love. A brother or sister for Johnny.

Next to having a healthy baby, the only thing she could wish for was Joe's love. But whether Joe was pleased or angry about the baby, she would try her best to be the most wonderful wife in the world. She would be both understanding and supportive. Maybe then his love would follow.

SABLE DROPPED JOHNNY OFF at the nursery school she had enrolled him in so he'd have playmates, then returned to the ranch to wait for Joe. She had just finished seasoning a roast when she heard the car door slam. She tensed in anticipation.

Joe was home. Wiping her suddenly slick palms on her slacks, she pretended to check the oven dials. She told herself it was only natural that she would fear his reaction, both to her declaration of love and to the fact that he was to become a father. Nevertheless, she felt as though lightning sizzled down her spine.

Straightening, she faced the back door. One hand nervously checked to make sure her hair was still sleekly secure in its knot.

But when Joe appeared in the doorway, every word she had rehearsed flew out of her head. He wore a dark blue suit, his tanned skin in stark contrast to the white of his dress shirt. A maroon tie with a blue design dangled from his clenched fist.

"Hi." His voice held the smoothness of velvet and the golden heat of aged bourbon.

"Hi," was all she managed.

"You had the house painted."

"And the porch. It was my treat."

He didn't argue. "The same color."

"I thought you wouldn't notice as quickly."

"I knew I had good taste the first time." His blue eyes stared into hers, searching—for what? she wondered.

"You hired a maid."

He shrugged. "It's only once a week. I thought you could use the help."

She swallowed. "How was your trip?"

"One confrontation after another."

"Was it successful?"

He nodded, his eyes still pinning her down.

"And did you get what you wanted?"

"Almost."

She swallowed again. "What happened?"

He walked toward her, and she suddenly felt cornered, as if she were his prey.

When Joe stood in front of her, his eyes took in her strained expression, the dark circles under her eyes. The anxious biting of her lips.

He narrowed his eyes. "What happened here?"

Sable turned, placing the oven mitt on the counter. "Nothing much."

"Then why do you look as if you haven't slept in weeks?" He took one hand in his and turned it over, palm up. His thumb ran over the light calluses there. "You used to have the softest, most ladylike hands I'd ever seen," he mused.

She snatched her hand away, anger warring with her resolve to be nice. "Now I muck out stalls once a week and do housework for four people," she snapped. "How could you possibly expect soft hands?"

"You work too hard," he said gently. He touched her on the shoulders. Her bones were more prominent than before. "You've lost weight."

"Are you through categorizing my faults yet? Shall I help you?"

His gaze searched her face. She wanted to cry. Tears filmed her eyes, but she stoutly refused to let them fall or allow him to force her to look away. "What are they?" he asked.

She pushed back a loose strand of hair. "I'm rude, aloof, and right now I'm kind of crazy."

"I vote for all of the above."

"How can you not?" she asked crossly. "And I'm sure that if you look hard enough, you'll be able to find something else to complain about."

"There's nothing wrong with you. All I said was you needed more sleep and more help. I didn't know that my observations would open floodgates of bitterness." His voice was soft and teasing.

She stared up at him. He wasn't angry. He was still smiling in that wonderful, indulgent way he had.

Her mood changed abruptly. "I know. I'm not sure I always understand me, either."

"Right," he drawled. Then he pulled a fat, white envelope out of his coat pocket. "I need to discuss something with you right now."

"Yes." Sable took his hand and pulled him into the living room. "I need to talk to you, too. And I should go first." Sable sat down beside him on the couch, one leg curled under her as she leaned toward him.

For the first time since he'd walked in the door, Joe looked wary. "Let me begin—"

"No, I need to apologize, and that has to be done first."

Joe looked shocked. "For what?"

Sable looked down, still holding Joe's hand. His strong, tanned fingers were twined seductively around hers.

Then she gazed back into his eyes. "I married you for all the wrong reasons. I panicked."

His finger traced her cheek. "I know."

It was a sad statement, one filled with enough regret for both of them, and her heart sank.

"I'm sorry. Something happened to Talia and me when we were kids, and I allowed it to color my thinking."

"Talia told me about the custody battle, Sable. It had to be horrible for you both."

"You know all about it?" she asked in surprise.

He nodded. "It explained a lot, but it left my ego in shreds."

"Why?"

He shrugged, suddenly looking like a little boy embarrassed to be caught stealing penny candy. "I hoped you had more than one reason to marry me. That maybe you married me because you were attracted to me."

She tilted her head and stared at him, a question in her eyes and on her lips. "Did you like that idea?"

His grip tightened. "Yes."

"Yes, what?" she prodded, wanting, needing him to say he wanted her. Needed her. Loved her. She held her breath.

Joe sighed. "Yes, I liked the idea. I liked it more than I can tell you."

She was disappointed, but continued to press. "Why?"

"Before I get into that, I want you to have this," he said, holding out the fat envelope.

Sable stared at him, then at the envelope. With shaky fingers she accepted it, then carefully lifted the flap. She pulled out the sheaf of papers and cautiously unfolded them. Her eyes widened. Sable glanced at Joe, then back down at the papers again. "These are Ahab's papers."

Joe nodded.

"They're made out to me."

He nodded again.

"I don't understand."

"Ahab will be worth a million dollars by the time his prize monies and stud fees are calculated over his lifetime. I'm paying you back for your investment in the track."

"But I didn't invest. I gave you the money in exchange for a marriage certificate."

"And I'm giving you back the money." His voice was patient. "This way we're even. The debt is paid."

"And the marriage?"

His smile disappeared. "Is still a marriage. And if you're willing to try again, I think we might be able to make it work, Sable. I just don't want the money to be an obstacle to working out our problems."

"I didn't think it was."

He smiled sadly. "Don't lie, honey. We both know it was. It was the wall between us. Now it's down, and we can concentrate on ourselves."

"You love that horse."

"And I still do. Just because he's yours doesn't mean I won't see him or watch him race. But you'll receive whatever money he makes." A hint of a smile crinkled his eyes, bringing out the tiny dimple on his cheek, Sable noticed. "As well as his feed and vet bills."

She loved his easy teasing. Her hand cradled his jaw. "And now what happens, Joe?" she questioned softly.

Her husband looked away. "This is your apology, remember? I'll tell you what I have to say after you finish."

"I want to hear it now."

"You insisted on going first."

Sable laughed. He'd given away far more than he thought. "Okay." She took both his hands in hers. "I'm sorry about the beer episode. It wasn't fair of me to judge the men. I had nothing to go on but a built-in prejudice against beer."

"I accept your apology on their behalf."

"And I'm sorry about shouting at you the morning, the time—"

"—the morning I climbed into your bed and Talia found us?" he finished dryly.

Sable nodded. "I wasn't able to cope with the changes, so I took it out on you."

"I should have seen that. But I wanted you so much, I didn't stop to think," he told her, his voice filled with regret. "If I hadn't pushed so hard, we might still be sharing our nights."

She looked back up at him. "I love you."

The silence hung between them, as tense as a bowstring. His grip tightened, painfully so.

Then he dropped her hands and reached for her shoulders. "Say it again," he demanded.

Sable swallowed the lump in her throat. "I love you." Then she remembered their child and her resolve returned. Despite her failings, she took care of those she loved. The children were hers. It would be up to Joe to decide whether he wanted to be a part of their lives, as well.

She tilted her chin defiantly. "I love you!" she declared for the third time, her voice stronger now.

"Since when? Since you kicked me out of your bed? Since you screamed at me in my office? Since you snubbed me in my own home? When?"

"Since all of that," she said quietly. "I wasn't supposed to love you. I didn't want to. But I do."

His triumphant laughter shook the rafters. "I knew it! I knew you had to care for me, or you wouldn't have made love with me."

"Well, you don't have to be so vocal about it," Sable told him, pulling away. "It isn't nice to crow."

He leaned forward and kissed her. It was meant to be an old-fashioned buss, but turned into a wonderful, heartwarming, soul-talking kiss.

His mouth never leaving hers, he wrapped his arms around her waist and pulled her into his lap. She clung to him, her fingers losing themselves in his dark hair. His tongue found its way in and captured hers. Somewhere deep inside, Sable realized she was with Joe in their home, but as long as she was in his arms, she knew she was in heaven.

He held her so close, she thought she'd never lose the imprint of his body. But she didn't want it any other way. Joe was gruff, sometimes rough, sometimes tender—and she loved him in every way possible.

Joe rested his lips on her forehead, his warm breath soothing her brow. "We need to cancel that damn contract and write up a new one. You keep your money, I keep mine. Everything else belongs to us. No five-year plans. No other rules. We'll make them up as we go along."

Sable pulled away and stared up at him. Now it was her turn to demand. "Say it."

His eyes burned into hers, but she ignored their message. "Say it!"

His throat constricted, so that his words came out in a whisper. "I love you."

"Again," she demanded softly, finally allowing herself to dream.

His hands circled her face. The last hesitation faded from his eyes. "I love you. Completely. Forever. I love you, Sable LaCroix Lombardi."

She grinned. "It's about time you earned your silver tongue, you devil."

He clasped her close to him again. "You're my world, Sable." His voice teased her hair. "That scares the hell out of me."

"Me, too," she admitted.

"You're staying with me."

"Yes." She bestowed a butterfly kiss upon his white-shirt-covered chest.

"Joe?"

"Mmm?" he asked, his lips touching her hair as his hand stroked her back.

She couldn't resist the age-old question. "When did you know that you loved me?"

His answer came immediately. "When you stood in the doorway of my barn and proposed to me."

She lifted her head and stared at him. "But that was the first day we met!"

Laughter rumbled in his chest. "I know."

"When did you decide it was love?"

"When I heard you shouting at me as I went down in the racetrack elevator. You yelled something about me running away. It dawned on me then that I never did that, unless I was afraid of the love being offered. Of a happy ever after."

She stroked his cheek. "You didn't want to believe?"

His hand covered hers, and he brought her palm to his lips. "On the contrary. I've been searching for love all my life, but when I met you, I was afraid to believe in it, for fear you'd never return my love."

"Believe," she whispered, teasing his lips with hers. "Believe, my darling."

He sighed. "All the way home I was afraid you wouldn't be here."

"Where would I be?"

"I was afraid you'd leave me. I didn't want to know that. I wanted to pretend you were here, even if you weren't."

His words wrapped themselves around her heart and squeezed. She'd read all the signals wrong. They both bore childhood scars. "Oh, darling," she murmured. And then she remembered her secret. At least she knew now that Joe would be happy about the baby. No man could need so much love and not be happy.

The drone of a plane caught Joe's attention, and he pulled her up with him as they went to the front door and down the steps to the yard.

"Look," he said, pointing upward. "This was supposed to be my surprise. I thought if I let the world know how much I loved you, there was a chance you might take pity on me and love me back."

Sable stared at the plane above, which was skywriting *I Love You, Sable* in big script letters.

She had her storybook romance. She'd found her hero. Sometimes real life did resemble romantic fiction. Sometimes real life was even better than the love stories.

She hugged Joe, laughing in delight. "I don't believe it! Joe Lombardi is a romantic!" She stared at him, then again at the words in the pale blue sky. She wanted to cry as much as she was laughing. It touched her so deeply to think that this man cared enough to announce it to the world, or at least to the world of Conroe, Texas. And that this same man had such a hard time forming the words!

"You have a vivid imagination, husband mine," she whispered into his ear as she gave him one more hug. The plane had gone, and the writing began drifting away on the breeze, but the man who'd made it possible was still here with her.

"Then let's play another game of Let's Pretend, darling," Joe said, a wicked gleam in his eye. "We'll start all over again. Just as if this were the first time we met. But this time we'll do all the right things." He kissed the shell of her ear. "Make a fresh start."

"A fresh start," she repeated, loving the sound of the words. She grinned. It was going to be hard to explain a fresh start when there was a month-old life curled beneath her heart. "Joe? I have something to tell you, darling."

"No, it's my turn," he told her. "I've asked Jonathan's grandparents to baby-sit, so we can have a honeymoon."

Her mind went blank. "The LaCroix?"

He nodded. "I knew we needed time alone together, without any distractions, so I asked them if they wanted to take care of Jonathan and Talia while we're away. They said yes—with a few conditions."

"What conditions?" Sable asked warily.

He gave her a hug. "Don't worry. They're coming here to stay for a week. But they're also bringing a maid and a cook."

"Of course!" she chortled. "What else would they do?"

"Well, they did want to bring a handyman and a nanny as well, but I talked them out of that."

"How?"

"I told them they would have to buy a recreational vehicle for the two women to stay in, and that if they also brought a nanny, they might miss the real experience of learning to know Jonathan."

"What about the handyman?"

"I told them we had twelve handymen in the bunkhouse, who also double as baby-sitters in emergencies." He looked very satisfied with himself.

"And when is this trip to take place? Where are we going?"

"We're having a honeymoon in Ixtapa, Mexico. A friend of mine has a very secluded villa there." He frowned. "But we can't go for another week. I can't get away until the track opens."

"Is it far from the ocean?" she asked, thinking of a bikini that wouldn't quite fit by that time.

"Yes. About two hundred miles as the crow flies."

She dropped a kiss onto his bottom lip. "Never mind. What your lady needs is you. Alone."

Joe slipped one hand under her knees, the other around her back, and lifted her into his arms. "Let me explain what your man needs, lady. He's into anatomy these days, and he'd like to do a little studying."

Joe strode through the front door and down the hall toward his bedroom. Sable wrapped her arms around his neck and let him have his way.

"I thought we were pretending that we're meeting for the first time?" she asked, dropping kisses onto his neck and chest. "That would make this our first date, yet you're heading for the bedroom. What kind of a woman do you think I am?"

"You're my woman," he declared. His voice was low and filled with need. "It's my game, and I'm setting the rules. I'm pretending this is a one-night stand. Forever."

"Okay, big fella," she murmured against the curve of his neck. "But I expect to get my money's worth."

His chuckle echoed through the hall. "Honey, you don't know it, but that's exactly what I had in mind."

She laughed, a husky sound that was almost a purr. "That's forever," she confirmed.

"Right," he answered, finally allowing her feet to touch the ground. His hands went straight to her blouse buttons. With intense dedication, he applied himself to the task of undressing her.

"And when I'm finished with that, I'll begin lessons in teaching you how to drink beer. You have to sip it, smell the bouquet, test the temperature of it on your tongue. It's an art."

"Kiss me, you nut."

"With pleasure, my love. With pleasure." And then words became deeds.

There was suddenly plenty of time to tell him all the things she wanted to share.

After all, they had the rest of their lives. . . .

11

JOE PLACED a soft kiss on the nape of Sable's neck. They stood in a darkened corner of the far, second-story balcony, seeking a temporary retreat from the revelers. A twenty-four-piece orchestra took up one section of the grassy knoll by the pond. Fireworks painted the night sky with glorious streaks of color. Tuxedoed waiters wound through the crowd with silver trays filled with glasses of the finest champagne.

Racing at the Bluebonnet Racetrack would begin tomorrow.

"Talia was certainly excited tonight," Joe commented, his warm breath brushing her cheek. He stood behind her, allowing her to rest against him.

Sable chuckled. "I'm not sure if it was because she received a letter from Vassar, or because she's celebrating here with Mike."

"Mike will be very gentlemanly with her. You aren't worried, are you?"

"No. She's much too young for anything permanent. Especially now, with college waiting in the wings." Sable just hoped Mike could hold up under Talia's assault.

"Happy?" he murmured. His hands clasped her waist to pull her closer to the leanness of his body. She rested her head on his shoulder and stared into the softness of the dark.

"More than I can say."

"Ready for a week at that villa?"

"As long as you're there."

His lips touched her temple. "As soon as the balloons are released, we'll leave," he promised.

The balloons had been Sable's idea. Tucked inside five hundred of them were free passes to the upper gallery to watch the opening day's races.

Sable had a balloon tied to her wrist. She turned in his arms, facing him. "You have to pop your balloon first," she said.

"I thought it was a souvenir."

"No," she corrected softly. "This is a very special balloon. It will reveal your future."

Joe smiled indulgently, popped the balloon and caught the folded piece of white paper that fell from it. Still smiling, he unfolded the paper and tilted it toward the light.

Your wife will bear a child, to be born in the spring. You will live happily ever after.

His blue eyes delved into hers. "Is this a joke?"

She shook her head. Was he thrilled at the thought of becoming a father? Or did he feel cheated because they wouldn't have time alone before they began their own family?

"Are you sure?"

She nodded.

His smile lighted up the darkness that surrounded them. His laugh was deep and honest and full of the wonders of life. His arms encircled her, pulling her close to his warmth. "A child. Our child."

Her heart sang. "Our child," she confirmed.

Joe leaned back and stared into her upturned face. "Are you happy?"

"Yes," she said simply. "It's what I've always wanted."

He kissed the tip of her nose, his hands so light on her waist that she could hardly feel them. "Then we'll have a dozen."

"How about a compromise?"

"Six, then," he amended, pulling her toward him once more. "With Talia and Jonathan that will make eight. A nice round number."

"And we'll live happily ever after?" she teased.

His smile was replaced by an expression of sincerity. "Honey, I pray so. We're damn well going to try."

"We'll make it work," she promised. "We have luck on our side."

"Really?"

She nodded sagely. "After all, luck brought me to you when I was buying a groom. It certainly wouldn't dare desert me now, when I found a husband."

Joe chuckled. Now that the debt was paid, the money seemed such a small matter. And yet that money had given them the one thing they had wanted—each other.

A loud cheer roared around them. Six nets, filled with balloons, had just opened; the bright lights of the track allowed the spectators to watch their multicolored ascent.

Joe and Sable stood quietly on the second-floor balcony. His hand slid across the slick fabric of her full-length sheath and covered her still flat stomach.

Sable leaned back, her heart filled with contentment. For the rest of her life she would remember this moment and the feeling of completeness that encompassed it. His touch was so gentle, so sweet against her flesh. She wanted more.

"I won't break, you know," she told him. "I didn't break last night. Or the night before."

"And you won't break tonight, either," Joe promised. "But just in case, perhaps we'd better grab the limo now and head for home. I'll need to take my time making love to you. I certainly can't rush with you in such a delicate condition."

"You're absolutely right," she said, taking his hand in hers. "Let's go."

"In a hurry?" he inquired with a chuckle.

"Yes," she declared firmly, tossing the words over her shoulder. "To live life. With you."

"Forever," he muttered, swinging her around to fill the curve of his arms as he kissed her once more.

The spotlights caught them, the balloons framed them. But Joe didn't care.

Finally he was somebody's hero.

And he'd spend the rest of his life proving it.

Take 4 bestselling love stories FREE

Plus get a FREE surprise gift!

Special Limited-time Offer

Harlequin Reader Service®

Mail to

In the U.S.	In Canada
3010 Walden Avenue	P.O. Box 609
P.O. Box 1867	Fort Erie, Ontario
Buffalo, N.Y. 14269-1867	L2A 5X3

YES! Please send me 4 free Harlequin Temptations® novels and my free surprise gift. Then send me 4 brand-new novels every month, which I will receive months before they appear in bookstores. Bill me at the low price of $2.39* each—a savings of 26¢ apiece off cover prices. There are no shipping, handling or other hidden costs. I understand that accepting the books and gift places me under no obligation ever to buy any books. I can always return a shipment and cancel at any time. Even if I never buy another book from Harlequin, the 4 free books and the surprise gift are mine to keep forever.

*Offer slightly different in Canada—$2.39 per book plus 49¢ per shipment for delivery. Sales tax applicable in N.Y.

342 BPA ZDHU (CAN)

142 BPA MDX5 (US)

Name _____ (PLEASE PRINT)

Address _____ Apt. No. _____

City _____ State/Prov. _____ Zip/Postal Code _____

This offer is limited to one order per household and not valid to present Harlequin Temptation® subscribers. Terms and prices are subject to change.

© 1990 Harlequin Enterprises Limited

PASSPORT TO ROMANCE
SWEEPSTAKES RULES

1. **HOW TO ENTER:** To enter, you must be the age of majority and complete the official entry form, or print your name, address, telephone number and age on a plain piece of paper and mail to: Passport to Romance, P.O. Box 9056, Buffalo, NY 14269-9056. No mechanically reproduced entries accepted.

2. All entries must be received by the CONTEST CLOSING DATE, DECEMBER 31, 1990 TO BE ELIGIBLE.

3. **THE PRIZES:** There will be ten (10) Grand Prizes awarded, each consisting of a choice of a trip for two people from the following list:
   i) London, England (approximate retail value $5,050 U.S.)
   ii) England, Wales and Scotland (approximate retail value $6,400 U.S.)
   iii) Carribean Cruise (approximate retail value $7,300 U.S.)
   iv) Hawaii (approximate retail value $9,550 U.S.)
   v) Greek Island Cruise in the Mediterranean (approximate retail value $12,250 U.S.)
   vi) France (approximate retail value $7,300 U.S.)

4. Any winner may choose to receive any trip or a cash alternative prize of $5,000.00 U.S. in lieu of the trip.

5. **GENERAL RULES:** Odds of winning depend on number of entries received.

6. A random draw will be made by Nielsen Promotion Services, an independent judging organization, on January 29, 1991, in Buffalo, NY, at 11:30 a.m. from all eligible entries received on or before the Contest Closing Date.

7. Any Canadian entrants who are selected must correctly answer a time-limited, mathematical skill-testing question in order to win.

8. Full contest rules may be obtained by sending a stamped, self-addressed envelope to: "Passport to Romance Rules Request", P.O. Box 9998, Saint John, New Brunswick, Canada E2L 4N4.

9. Quebec residents may submit any litigation respecting the conduct and awarding of a prize in this contest to the Régie des loteries et courses du Québec.

10. Payment of taxes other than air and hotel taxes is the sole responsibility of the winner.

11. Void where prohibited by law.

COUPON BOOKLET OFFER TERMS

To receive your Free travel-savings coupon booklets, complete the mail-in Offer Certificate on the preceeding page, including the necessary number of proofs-of-purchase, and mail to: Passport to Romance, P.O. Box 9057, Buffalo, NY 14269-9057. The coupon booklets include savings on travel-related products such as car rentals, hotels, cruises, flowers and restaurants. Some restrictions apply. The offer is available in the United States and Canada. Requests must be postmarked by January 25, 1991. Only proofs-of-purchase from specially marked "Passport to Romance" Harlequin® or Silhouette® books will be accepted. The offer certificate must accompany your request and may not be reproduced in any manner. Offer void where prohibited or restricted by law. LIMIT FOUR COUPON BOOKLETS PER NAME, FAMILY, GROUP, ORGANIZATION OR ADDRESS. Please allow up to 8 weeks after receipt of order for shipment. Enter quickly as quantities are limited. Unfulfilled mail-in offer requests will receive free Harlequin® or Silhouette® books (not previously available in retail stores), in quantities equal to the number of proofs-of-purchase required for Levels One to Four, as applicable.

OFFICIAL SWEEPSTAKES
ENTRY FORM

Complete and return this Entry Form immediately—the more Entry Forms you submit. the better your chances of winning!
- Entry Forms must be received by **December 31, 1990**
- A random draw will take place on **January 29, 1991**
- Trip must be taken by **December 31, 1991**

3-HT-1-SW

YES. I want to win a PASSPORT TO ROMANCE vacation for two! I understand the prize includes round-trip air fare, accommodation and a daily spending allowance

Name_____

Address_____

City_____ State_____ Zip_____

Telephone Number_____ Age_____

Return entries to: **PASSPORT TO ROMANCE**, P.O. Box 9056, Buffalo, NY 14269-9056

© 1990 Harlequin Enterprises Limited

COUPON BOOKLET/OFFER CERTIFICATE

Item	LEVEL ONE Booklet 1	LEVEL TWO Booklet 1 & 2	LEVEL THREE Booklet 1, 2 & 3	LEVEL FOUR Booklet 1, 2, 3 & 4
Booklet 1 = $100+	$100+	$100+	$100+	$100+
Booklet 2 = $200+		$200+	$200+	$200+
Booklet 3 = $300+			$300+	$300+
Booklet 4 = $400+	____	____	____	$400+
Approximate Total Value of Savings	$100+	$300+	$600+	$1,000+
# of Proofs of Purchase Required	4	6	12	18
Check One	____	____	____	____

Name_____

Address_____

City_____ State_____ Zip_____

Return Offer Certificates to: **PASSPORT TO ROMANCE**. P.O Box 9057 Buffalo. NY 14269-9057

Requests must be postmarked by **January 25, 1991**

ONE PROOF OF PURCHASE

3-HT-1

To collect your free coupon booklet you must include the necessary number of proofs-of-purchase with a properly completed Offer Certificate

© 1990 Harlequin Enterprises Limited

See previous page for details